"One of our angels disappeared in New York City. Using the mortal name of Wiley Boggs, he was sent down to spread Christmas cheer, something he does every year. But he hasn't been heard from since."

The other angel nodded sadly. "And we've been getting all kinds of reports, terrible reports. Because of his disappearance, the city is missing its traditional Christmas spirit."

Poppa's eyes widened in disbelief. New York City without Christmas spirit?

"Now, you were a police detective," the Arch Angel said. "Well, here's the deal...."

It Came Upon The Midnight Clear

MICKEY ROONEY

in

IT CAME UPON THE MIDNIGHT CLEAR

Introducing
SCOTT GRIMES
as Robbie Westin

Starring
BARRIE YOUNGFELLOW
GEORGE GAYNES
GARY BAYER
WILLIAM GRIFFIS
CHRISTINA PICKLES
HAMILTON CAMP
ELISHA COOK
NICHOLAS HORMANN
WYNN IRWIN
HECTOR ELIAS
BARBETTE TWEED
LEW HORN

and

ANNIE POTTS
as Cindy Mills

Special Appearance By
LLOYD NOLAN
as Monsignor Donoghue

Film Editor
JERROLD L. LUDWIG, A.C.E.

Art Directors
ROSS BELLAH
and CARL BRAUNGER

Director of Photography
DEAN CUNDEY

Music by
ARTHUR B. RUBINSTEIN

Produced by
FRANK CARDEA
&
GEORGE SCHENCK

Written by
GEORGE SCHENCK
&
FRANK CARDEA

Directed by
PETER H. HUNT

It Came Upon The Midnight Clear

Leonore Fleischer

BALLANTINE BOOKS • NEW YORK

Library of Congress Catalog Card Number:

ISBN 0-345-32163-4

Manufactured in the United States of America

First Edition: December 1984

It Came Upon The Midnight Clear

ONE

"DID YOU EVER HEAR BING CROSBY SINGing, 'I'm Dreaming of a *Green* Christmas'?" muttered Mike Halligan half to himself as he took out his already damp handkerchief and mopped his sweaty neck for the third time in five minutes. "No, and you never will, neither." He shook his head in discontent, and a scowl made his usually friendly Irish mug, with its snub nose and wide mouth, look old for a moment. And Mike Halligan wasn't old. Getting on, maybe; retired, maybe; and maybe a little less active, but anybody who called Mike Halligan old had to answer to Mike Halligan.

With an annoyed snort, he followed his daughter into the school auditorium. His daughter, one of the only three bright spots in this Mickey Mouse Los Angeles landscape with its crazy palm trees, all stalk and three leaves at the top, fifty feet off the ground . . . he was rambling again. Kate, his beloved daughter, and her two wonderful children—they were the only reason that he was here, living in L.A., instead of back in New York, where he belonged.

That, and because his darling Mary—may God give peace to her blessed, sweet soul—was resting in the ground. As usual, the thought of his wife of thirty-eight years, his Mary, who had been his life's companion and who was supposed to be growing old beside him, struck him like a blow in his gut, as though her death were yesterday and not nearly a year ago.

Alone in the world, retired from the police force, what was there for a man to do except move out to California to live with his only daughter, his only grandson, Robbie, and only granddaughter, Missy? Oh, yes, and his only son-in-law, too, although somehow Mike always had to remember to tack him on last, like the paper tail on the donkey in the game. Not that he had anything against Rick Westin. The man took good and loving care of Kate and the two kids; he behaved as any husband and father should. Still, there wasn't a lot of closeness between the two of them, because Mike could never understand why they couldn't all go back to live in New York, instead of out here, where the temperature was in the eighties just three days before Christmas. Mike had seen a sidewalk Santa in sunglasses and bermuda shorts! What kind of a Christmas was *this*?

Never mind, it was *going* to be a great Christmas. Taking Robbie to New York, to see the department store windows and the decorations, everybody smiling through blue lips, noses red with cold, snow in the air, swirling in lacy patterns around the skyscrapers, snow underfoot, white and beautiful for about three minutes, then turning to slush. Ah, even muddy slush was better than all this sunshine and beach. Ever hear, "Dashing through the *sand* in a one-horse open sleigh"? It hadn't been easy, persuading the Westins to part with Robbie for Christmas, but Kate had worked on Rick to let Poppa (that's what they called him out here) take Robbie, because the old man's heart was so set on it, and besides, who knew how much longer...?

Mike knew what they'd been talking about behind closed doors, that Poppa was geting old and probably wouldn't live that much longer, and why not indulge him a little, and what could possibly happen to the two of them? That would be Kate saying that. And Rick was probably saying, Well, the old guy is getting a little, you know, senile. Funny in the head, and how do we know we can trust him? And Kate saying, For Heaven's sake,

Rick, he's only sixty-five and he's a New York City police detective! And Rick saying: Not anymore he isn't; he's retired. Even so, Rick finally gave in; after all, it was only for a few days. Only for Christmas.

Christmas. A holy time in which the heart expands and grows roomy enough to fit even strangers into it. A time for shared smiles and public laughter. A time for the one you love best in the world to be with you to share the magic. A time to be home, where you belong.

Poppa no longer had the one he loved best in the world since his wife had died, but his heart had expanded and Robbie had come to fill it. There was a special relationship between those two, and if you saw them together, Mike all grinning and impish and playful, you might find it difficult to say which of them was the older. Poppa took on a new youthfulness with Robbie; the two of them spoke the same language.

Home to Poppa was still New York City, and Christmas meant midnight Mass at St. Patrick's Cathedral, and skating in Rockefeller Center, and the incredibly magical department store windows. His headquarters had been Midtown North, and every Christmastime he was out on the street, watching the happy, if frozen, faces of the people lining up to look into the windows at Altman's, Saks, and especially Lord and Taylor. Kids would hold their parents' hands with their mittens, and they would stare, their eyes round with wonder, at the elegant me-

chanical rabbits in velvet waistcoats dancing with rav-
ishingly beautiful cats in ball gowns, jewels in their fur.
Or Santa's Workshop, where cunning elves made Christmas presents with their little hammers and paintbrushes,
while outside, Dasher, Dancer, Prancer, and Rudolph
were being hitched to the sleigh. Santa would be putting
on his boots, his red suspenders pulled up over his long
johns, and Mrs. Claus, her hair tucked neatly up into a
bun, would be bringing him a thermos of hot cocoa for
the long journey. And all of these automated creatures
moved with such grace and precision! The animals at the
ball waltzed merrily to Strauss, tiaras twinkling; the
workshop bustled, and Santa groaned a little as his belly
got in the way of his boots. The windows were truly
miraculous, and the parents' eyes were as round and
staring as the childrens'.

Oh, the windows, the store windows! And the snow.
And the smiles, not often seen on New York faces except
at this time of the year. A different kind of feeling was
in the air now, a friendly, loving feeling, as the shoppers
bustled into the stores or dragged home bunches of fragrant pine or wreaths of stiff holly with red berries still
clinging to them, and long-needled green Christmas trees.
Even the tall office buildings, skyscrapers of steel, glass,
and stone, were beautiful. Giant stars and festoons of
light illuminated them, changing them into fifty-story
wonderlands; the Chrysler Building wore a diadem of

lights, and the top of the majestic Empire State Building glowed red and green for the holidays. If ever New York was beautiful, Christmas was that time. If ever New Yorkers were friendly to one another, even though strangers, Christmas was that time. If ever there was a time to be in New York City, Christmas was that time.

Poppa had been telling Robbie about all this, and the boy's eyes shone with eagerness; he couldn't wait to climb aboard that New York plane. Poppa had promised him snow, and Robbie had never seen snow. Not real snow, anyhow, although Aqualand put down fake snow every year around this time.

Robbie and Poppa had been going to see the Christmas sights in Los Angeles for a week now, because Kate and Robbie wanted Mike to see that it was possible to have Christmas in California, too. They drove down Wilshire Boulevard and Rodeo Drive to look at the windows, but Poppa just shook his head. Compared with New York? Forget it. They visited Santa's Village in the Mall, but the temperature hit ninety that day, and the Santa was dripping sweat inside his suit and beard, even though the air-conditioning was turned up high. Not too convincing. Robbie went ice-skating to Christmas music at the Laurel Plaza, but Poppa said that Rockefeller Center was a hundred times better. They saw quite a lot of Nativity scenes, but Poppa only reminded Kate of the Nativity at Radio City Music Hall, where he'd taken her every year when she was a little girl, and Kate had to agree that it was definitely the best.

The streets and boulevards were decorated to a fare-thee-well, but the glaring sunshine made the colors look somewhat tacky, and who ever heard of a holly wreath on a date palm tree? Only one tree made the slightest impression on Poppa, the big one at the Chandler Pavilion, decorated with thousands of lights and looking like a Christmas tree ought to. All the children went there, to the Music Center, to see the tree and the Nutcracker Suite, to hear the carolers and the minstrels, to watch the silent mimes, to eat the hot dogs and the popcorn.

After Thanksgiving, Kate, Robbie, and Missy had taken Poppa to the Christmas Lane Parade, and there had been marching bands, and Hollywood stars riding on the floats, but Poppa sighed out loud, remembering the Macy's Parade, with its huge balloons swaying building-high over the windy streets, Popeye and Bullwinkle and Snoopy.

It's not that Poppa hated Los Angeles, you understand. Grudgingly, he would admit that having warm weather all year round wasn't so terrible, that seeing bright flowers in December had its points. Actually, the red poinsettias that were in bloom everywhere you looked *were* a touch of genuine Christmas cheer. They were beautiful, a living Christmas card, all red and green and lush. It was the only thing that Poppa could concede was better there than in New York, those flaming banks of poinsettias.

But the Christmas trees that people took home and set up! Well, they just floored Poppa. At this time of year, Christmas tree lots would spring up everywhere—in every empty lot, in every gas station, just about on every corner. If they sold real trees, evergreen trees of real pine or spruce, after a couple of days in the broiling sun those trees were a pathetic sight, drying out, needles turning brown. But there weren't too many of those. What people bought were flocked trees. Every lot had a little shed on it where the flocking was done, where green trees were sprayed with this fluffy, gaudy flocking and sold to eager buyers. Most of the flocked trees were white, but signs proclaimed that here you could find every color in the rainbow, including purple, and a few that weren't in the rainbow, like gold and silver. Some of the favorite colors besides white were pink, blue, and even (and here Poppa shuddered) *green*, just like the real thing. Only nobody wanted the real thing. What they wanted was to drive home from the beach with their sneakers full of sand, pull up at a gas station, and get their tanks filled with super unleaded while they picked out the tree of their choice and had it flocked in fuchsia with purple polka dots. Poppa could hardly believe his eyes.

He was counting the hours before he and Robbie were

on that eastbound jet, and still praying silently for snow, as he and Kate took their seats in the half-filled school auditorium. This was the last day of school before the Christmas vacation; all the parents and friends of parents had been invited to the holiday concert. Poppa sat impatiently through what seemed like endless piano solos and violin cadenzas played by inexpert, childish hands, but when the fourth-grade class filed onto the stage for the finale, bumping into one another and stepping on one another's toes, Poppa's eyes lit up with pleasure. He recognized the red bangs and the freckled nose of the person he loved most in the world. Robbie.

Kate, bless her darlin' heart, looked very much like his late Mary, rest her soul, only taller and slimmer, a handsome woman. But Robbie looked exactly like Mike himself had as a boy of nine, red-haired and merry-faced, with an Irish grin that came straight to you and warmed you up. Just the sight of him took Mike back to his own boyhood in Flatbush, Brooklyn. He wished now he had his big bag of marbles, the clear puries and the powerful shooters that he'd won in so many street games. He'd give them all to Robbie. Kids today didn't shoot marbles, though. They shot aliens down out of space ships in video arcades.

Now the music teacher was shushing the giggling and whispering boys and girls. She blew a note on her pitch pipe, and a hush fell over the fourth grade and the audience. Suddenly, fifty childish voices broke into the sweetness of a Christmas carol, and the song rose and filled the auditorium with its beauty.

"It came upon the midnight clear," sang the children, "that glorious song of old. . . ." Poppa felt the sudden sting of tears behind his eyes; it was his favorite carol. In the back row of the carolers, he could see Robbie, mouth open in song. Mike reached into his pocket and pulled out his little flash camera.

Kate smiled to herself at her father's enthusiasm as he rose to his feet and began proudly snapping pictures of Robbie. She also smiled because she could hear Robbie's voice; it was unmistakable, the only one in the group so horribly off-key. Actually, he wasn't supposed to be singing at all; he had been placed in the back row deliberately, to be a "listener." Robbie was only supposed to be mouthing the words. He must have been caught up in the excitement of the performance to give voice like that. Kate could see the music teacher wincing a little as she glared at Robbie, and her own grin widened. Robbie's voice was something only a doting grandfather could love. Only Poppa.

Poppa was snapping away, a big smile making his sixty-five-year-old face as young as a lad's. He, too, could tell Robbie's voice from the others—who couldn't?—but to Poppa it was music. "Peace on the earth, good will to men, from Heaven's all-gracious

King . . ." croaked Robbie, and the music teacher's eyes rolled up in despair.

All over the auditorium, flashbulbs went off as proud parents and grandparents recorded this memorable occasion, but nobody took more pictures than Poppa. As the fourth-graders finished their carol, the concert came to an end, with Robbie's tuneless squawk marring an otherwise perfect finale. Poppa, reluctant to leave the scene of his grandson's triumph, trailed Kate out of the coolness of the auditorium and into the humidity of the scorching afternoon. The wet handkerchief came out of the pocket again as they crossed the school parking lot.

"What a kid!" Enthusiastically, Mike mopped at his streaming face. "His voice just stood out from all the rest!"

Kate bit her lip to keep from laughing out loud. "It sure did" was all she'd allow herself to say, not wanting to spoil her father's pleasure.

But Poppa hadn't been a cop for all those years for nothing. He caught the dryness of her tone and saw the corners of her mouth suppressing laughter. "Ahhhhh, I thought he was great," he grumbled.

Now the corners of Kate's mouth tugged a smile up. "You're not prejudiced, are you?" she teased as she inserted her key into the station wagon door.

Poppa climbed in beside her, into the roomy front seat

of the Chevy Malibu. He and his daughter shared a moment of comfortable silence as they exchanged smiles. Ah, she was so much like her mother, this little girl of his, and he loved her so dearly!

They drove to a large corner lot on Ventura Boulevard, which was filled with multicolored flocked trees, while other trees, their branches drying out and brittle, waited their turn to be colored to order.

Poppa frowned at the stacks of pink and blue, silver and gold trees as he made his way through them behind Kate. A salesman was already hurrying up.

"May I help you?" He had one of those California have-a-nice-day smiles.

"Oh, yes," said Kate. "I want something full. About six or seven feet."

"The larger trees are over here." The salesman turned to lead the way, and Kate followed, but Poppa lagged behind. He was watching in disbelief as a bright-pink Christmas tree was sold to a lady carrying an apricot poodle. They were lashing the tree to the roof of a burgundy-colored Mercedes whose license plate was MUNNY. Poppa just couldn't figure it. Couldn't these people see how absurd these things were, how different from the spirit of Christmas? Deck the halls with boughs of flocking? Giving a snort of disgust, Mike wandered over to the section of the lot where the trees were being sprayed.

He watched in silence for a minute as a young man,

stripped to the waist and sweating heavily, sprayed a tree cerulean blue. Then, unable to take it a minute more, Poppa exploded.

"Why are you spraying that junk on those trees?" he demanded indignantly.

The boy looked up from his work, surprised. "Huh?"

"It's ridiculous! Christmas trees are supposed to be *green*!"

The boy scratched his head. "Hey, no problem, mister!" He gave Poppa a broad grin. "You want it green, we can spray it green for you. Take only a few minutes."

But Poppa had already turned angrily away and gone off to find Kate. He discovered her on the other side of the lot, looking with approval at a large, dazzling tree flocked blindingly white.

"What do you think?" she asked as Poppa came into view.

The old man shook his head. "I think you've gone California on me, Kate. This hot weather's gotten to you." He grimaced at the glittering tree. "A *painted* tree?"

Kate sighed. "The hot weather hasn't gotten to me, Dad. It's gotten to the trees," she explained patiently. "The salesman says they've all dried out, and the flocking keeps the needles from falling off."

Mike just grunted, eyeing the tree with disdain.

"Besides," continued Kate, "Missy's always wanted a white flocked tree."

Shrugging, Poppa relented. "Well, I hope you enjoy

it. . . . It doesn't matter to me, 'cause I'm not going to be here." One more time his thoughts turned happily to New York City with Robbie, to the joys of showing him all the wonderful Christmas sights they'd been talking about, and once again he asked God to make it snow so that a little California boy could have his first white Christmas.

School let out an hour early on the last day before the Christmas break, and Robbie Westin sped out the door as though shot from a bow. Hot on his sneakered heels was his best friend, Scotty Williams. They raced down the front steps together, through the parking lot and out the gate into freedom. Their nine-year-old hands were filled with the cards for their families that they'd made in class, with clay, crayons, craft paper and Magic Markers. All around them, their classmates shouted and waved their good-byes, and Robbie and Scotty yelled back, waving the best way they could, encumbered by the paper and clay.

"You're so lucky!" Scott gave Robbie a look of pure envy. "Going to New York with your grandfather."

"Yeah!" Robbie's proud grin revealed a few crucially missing teeth, spaces not yet filled in by the grownup set. "He says he wants to show me what Christmas is really like. Snow and Radio City and skating and everything!"

"Wish I were going with you. It sure sounds like fun."

"You're gonna have a good time in Palm Springs," Robbie assured his friend, although he didn't believe it himself.

But the other boy shook his head. "Not like you. I mean, it's just you and your grandfather. And he's so insane. Just like a little kid. Me," he whined, "I gotta go with my whole family."

As loyal a friend as he was, Robbie was also human, and he couldn't resist rubbing it in, just a little.

"Poppa said he and I are gonna stay up as late as we want, eat whatever we want, go wherever we want. . . ."

"Stop it!" Pained, Scotty jammed his Christmas cards over his ears. "I don't want to hear any more. You're makin' me jealous. You're going to New York City with a guy who's a real police detective, and I'm only goin' to dumb old Palm Springs. Well, Palm Springs isn't so bad, I suppose, but I gotta share a room with my mother's aunt. And she's one of those little old blue-haired things who're always pinching your cheek."

Robbie knew the kind, and he couldn't help grinning. Boy, did he feel sorry for Scotty! He also felt a little guilty, because Scotty had been his really truly best friend before Poppa had moved out here after Grandma died. I mean, they'd been in Little League together and everything. But somehow Robbie and Poppa had grown to love each other so much that now, even though he still referred to Scott as his "best friend," it wasn't quite true anymore. Poppa was Robbie's best friend in the world; he could tell Poppa anything—his deepest thoughts, even some of his fears—and his grandfather never laughed at him but always had something quiet and loving to say that made Robbie feel better. And Poppa was so smart! Part of it was because the old man had been a cop for such a long time, and then a detective for a long time—he'd even let Robbie wear his gold badge for a whole day once—but it seemed as though Poppa knew a whole lot more about the world than even Dad. And he never was too busy to teach Robbie things. Because he was retired and didn't have to go to work anymore, he had a lot of time to kill, and he liked nothing better than to kill it with Robbie.

Yes, Rob had come to love Poppa as much as he loved his mother and father, and a whole lot more than he loved Missy, that stuck-up fourteen-year-old who thought she was so special!

The Westins lived in a ranch-style house on a pleasant but ordinary street typical of the San Fernando Valley. Like most of the houses on the street, it had a split-level shape, a two-car garage, a little breezeway, which the developers rather pompously called "the lanai," an outdoor barbecue grill, and a couple of avocado trees in front. Unlike most of the other houses on the street, the Westins' house didn't have its outdoor Christmas lighting up yet. That's because Rick Westin, Dad, had been working late at the office and coming home too tired to think about it. Maybe this weekend.

Not that the Westins did an elaborate job of lighting. The Robinsons down the block had a life-size Santa on their roof every year, with four reindeer. The Kellys featured a huge lit-up Nativity scene, complete with manger, donkeys, Wise Men, camels, kneeling angels, Mary, Joseph, and the infant Jesus in a plastic crèche. But the Westin house was annually illuminated only by a few simple strings of colored lights following the outlines of the roof and the front door. It was understated, yet very pretty; the house was outlined by a soft glow.

So near leaving for New York, Poppa had caught the L.A. Christmas spirit and decided that today was the day. Rick Westin or no Rick Westin, the lights were going up. He'd already dragged the tall wooden ladder out of the garage and propped it against the overhang of the house. Now he was struggling with the heavy box of Christmas lights. They weighed a ton; Poppa's chest hurt and his legs wobbled as he carried the carton out of the garage.

As he set the box down beside the ladder and rubbed the sweat off his clammy forehead, Poppa saw the mailman, dressed in a short-sleeved regulation shirt and blue shorts, coming toward him across the lawn of the house next door. The sight made the old man smile.

"Hiya, Freddy. Hope you got my pension check."

Freddy extended a thick pack of mail, most of it in card-size envelopes. "It's right on top, Mr. Halligan. When are you and Robbie leaving?"

Poppa picked up the long windowed envelope with the government seal and gave it a smacking kiss. "Tomorrow. And I need every cent of this, because I'm going to show that kid the time of his life."

"I'm sure you will," said the mailman, heading off to his next delivery.

"Have a merry Christmas, Freddy," Poppa called after him.

"You, too."

As he climbed up the ladder with the tangled string of lights, Poppa felt a powerful burst of happiness. He had the money. Tomorrow was the day. Everything was going to be wonderful. It was even gonna snow; Poppa was certain of it. It was good to be alive.

He reached up to string the first light on the first eye-hook and the burst of happiness in his heart changed suddenly to a burst of agony. Pain coursed through his chest, around his ribs, up his left arm, and into his left shoulder, like a hot knife tearing him apart. Poppa grabbed at his chest, his face going white. He knew what that pain was; he'd seen too many others going like this.

"No," he whispered in agony. "Please, God, not now . . ."

The heart attack seized Mike Halligan in its relentless

claws and tumbled him down the ladder. He lay on the ground, very still, very pale, scarcely breathing.

ROBBIE AND SCOTTY HAD REACHED THE CORNER WHERE they had to go their separate ways home. They waved at each other as they parted, and Robbie turned to yell back to Scott that he'd send him a postcard of the Statue of Liberty. But a passing fire department rescue squad truck was rushing past with sirens wailing at top volume, so the boy's words were drowned out and Scott never heard them.

The siren kept sounding in Robbie's ears as he walked the short block to his house. Rounding the corner, he stopped in surprise, and the surprise changed instantly to uncertainty and alarm. Parked in front of his own house was the rescue unit, its red lights flashing an emergency.

The front door to the house was open, and Robbie headed for it at a dead run, his heart in his mouth. He never noticed the ladder or the string of lights hanging limply from one hook. Running into the house, he looked around wildly.

A white flocked tree had been set up in the living room, but no decorations had been hung on it yet. Robbie stepped back out into the hall just as a young paramedic in a white jacket came running past him and out the front door.

"Robbie!"

The boy turned. His sister was coming toward him, tears streaming down her face. Missy crying? *Missy?*

Apprehension gripped Robbie tightly as he saw that Missy's tears were real, that his sister's eyes were red with weeping.

"Missy! What's going on?" he gasped.

"It's Poppa. . . . He's had a heart attack or something." The girl faltered, wiping at her wet face with her hand. "He was putting up the Christmas lights by himself. Mom *told* him to wait for Dad, but . . . but . . ." and she broke into fresh tears.

Robbie took a step forward and was almost knocked down by the paramedic, who was coming back into the house on the run, lugging an oxygen tank complete with hose and face mask. The boy followed him down the hall to Poppa's bedroom, but the door opened and Mom came out, her face pale and frightened. The second paramedic, an older man, came out behind her, and he just shook his head silently at the oxygen tank. It wasn't needed now.

Tears spilled silently down Kate's cheeks as she drew her son and daughter into her arms. "They couldn't save him," she said, her voice choking with sobs. "I can't believe it. An hour ago he was so . . . h—h—happy and full of life. . . ." The sobs rose up in her throat to stifle her words.

Missy cried more loudly and tightened her arms about

her mother's waist, but Robbie broke away from them.

"Poppa! Poppa!" he cried out. None of this was real. It couldn't be real.

Running past the paramedics, pushing them as though they were nothing, he barged into his grandfather's room. His grandfather lay on his bed, his shirt pulled open at the collar, his eyes closed. There was no sign of breathing, and no color in the old man's face. He looked as though he'd been carved out of wax.

Robbie stopped dead in his tracks, staring at Poppa. It wasn't possible. Poppa *couldn't* be dead. They were going to New York tomorrow, just the two of them, and there was going to be snow, and Radio City . . . and . . .

Taking one step closer, and then another, Robbie's eyes never leaving the old man's face, the boy felt fear beginning to swell inside of him; he'd never seen a dead person before. And this was his best friend in the whole world, his grandfather. Poppa.

Belief was beginning to form, to grow. Tears sprang to the boy's eyes as the finality of the realization began to sink in. But it wasn't total, not yet.

"Poppa," Robbie whispered, inching closer to the still figure on the bed. He held out the handmade Christmas card, offering it tentatively to his grandfather. "I made this for you, Poppa."

He held the card close to the old man's face, to the unseeing eyes. It was a piece of white construction paper bordered in red and green Crayola. The drawing was a nine-year-old's version of heaven, a boy and his grandfather walking together down a street lined with wobbly skyscrapers. Snow was falling on them, big white flakes of it. New York City at Christmas.

The tears were coming fast now, spilling out of Robbie's eyes and down his freckled cheeks. But still he held the card out to his dead grandfather; still he talked to him, hoping vainly that by his words he could make the old man sit up, talk back to him, get off that bed, be *alive*.

"The art teacher told us to draw a holiday scene," he whispered through his tears. "It's you and me in New York. . . ."

Now he had to break off, because he was crying too hard to continue.

The older paramedic came into the room and laid a gentle hand on Robbie's shoulder.

"Son, it would be better if—"

But the boy turned on him savagely, kicking and hitting him with small, hard fists. "It's your fault!" shrieked Robbie, his voice filled with pain. "Why didn't you save him? Why did he have to die?"

The paramedic made no effort to avoid the boy's punches, realizing that the child needed to externalize his pain, to get it out of his system. He'd seen so much of this hurt when life-saving efforts failed; death seemed to be even more painful for those who were left behind.

"Robbie, Robbie . . ." Kate came into the room, reaching for her son, pulling him away from the paramedic, enfolding him. She turned the boy away from the bed so that he would no longer see the unmoving figure of Poppa.

"It's no one's fault, darling," she told him as she led him firmly from the room. "Nobody is to blame, Robbie. It's just what happened. That's all. Nobody could have prevented it. It just happened. . . ."

But the boy didn't hear his mother's words. He was crying too hard. Helpless, he allowed his mother to pull him out of the room, to close the door behind him, to try to give him comfort.

What comfort could there be, though, when Poppa lay there, dead on the bed? Where in the whole wide world could Robbie find comfort?

TWO

WHOA, THAT WAS A CLOSE CALL! POPPA GAVE his head a little shake to clear it, but he still felt pretty woozy. *Boy, I was sick as a dog there for a minute. Thought I'd be checking out for sure. Good warning, though. Gotta cut down on salt and get a little more exercise. Too much riding around on freeways; gotta take a three-mile walk every day from now on.* He felt better now, a lot better. The pain had totally disappeared, leaving him with an odd, lightheaded feeling, as though he were still in a dream he couldn't get out of. It actually seemed to him as though he were ascending a staircase spun out of golden light. *Stairway to heaven, ha ha.*

Around him, the light was hazy, diffused, and ethereal. Clouds billowed about the shaft, which mounted higher and higher into the heavens. *What a beautiful dream! Time to wake up now. Gotta take Robbie to New York. Gotta get off this bed and get my things packed. What bed? Wait a minute. Where's my bed? This isn't my room.* The column of light continued to climb, and Poppa climbed with it.

The sky was brighter now, and very clear. Around him the clouds were beginning to part, to reveal a most peculiar landscape. Poppa stared in disbelief.

A pair of shining gates with the patina of a string of pearls rose majestically from the sea of clouds. Cherubs, dimpled infants with rosy bare bottoms and iridescent wings, were polishing the gates with gauzy cloths, fluttering around it and bringing the portals to an even higher luster. Poppa blinked in disbelief. St. Peter's Gate? It couldn't be! He felt fine, terrific, never felt better in his life, in fact. Heaven's Gate? No way!

Now, for the first time, Poppa noticed that he wasn't alone. A long line of people were standing outside the Gate, silent, passive. The air was filled with the strangest music Mike Halligan had ever heard, gentle and commanding at the same time, otherworldly, but nobody except him appeared to be listening to it.

Poppa eyeballed the others standing on line; he seemed to be at the tail end of it. They were old people mostly, gray-haired and wrinkled. A large number of them were dressed in the pajamas or hospital gowns they had died in, but a few of them wore ordinary street clothing; they had died suddenly, without prior illness. Poppa glanced down at himself. He still had on the old shirt and khaki pants he was wearing when he'd started to hang the Christmas lights.

On line directly in front of him, an ancient, toothless man in a wrinkled hospital gown twisted around and spoke.

"Had to happen someday."

Distracted, Poppa looked blank. "Huh?"

"I knew I was a goner," cackled the ancient man. He must have been well into his eighties. "Told the doc. . . . Nothin' got me but old age. How about you?"

Poppa took one step backward, instinctively retreating from the words and their possible meaning. He was still totally disoriented; where was he? Who were all these people?

"I must be dreaming," he said aloud.

Just in front of the ancient man, a woman turned to Poppa. She was elderly, but not yet old, and her hair was still in curlers. She wore the kind of bathrobe that used to be called "a wrapper."

"No, you're not," she informed Poppa. "This isn't a dream. This is it!"

"I don't believe it!" It wasn't true! It *couldn't* be true! He wasn't ready!

The octogenarian displayed shrunken gums in a toothless smile. "Look, we're all old enough—"

"I'm not that old!" interrupted Poppa angrily.

"Then you should have taken better care of yourself," the housewife in the curlers told him smugly.

At this, a man further up the line wheeled around. Dressed in running shorts, a T-shirt, and Adidas, he couldn't have been more than thirty-five. "'Take care of yourself'?" he repeated in exasperation. "I was jogging five miles a day! What good did it do me?" He turned his back on them, his face stony with rage.

It was sinking in. Poppa was beginning to believe it. He was dead. This was, as the housewife had put it, "it." But that didn't make him like *it* any better. Not him, not Mike Halligan, one of the best of New York's Finest. *It*, huh? Well, we'll just see about that!

"You're gonna accept this?" he demanded of the passive others. He shook his head firmly. "Not me! I'm not going to walk through that gate!"

The old man just ahead of him shrugged bony, shrunken shoulders. "When your time comes, your time comes."

Easy for him to say! He's gotta be eighty-seven if he's a day! But I'm only sixty-five!! "I gotta get outta here," muttered Poppa, looking around him for some person...uh...angel...in authority.

There was one! An angel was hurrying by with a nervous look on his face. He was complete with wings and halo, but in his hands was a most incongruous object, a computer printout.

"Hey!" yelled Poppa. "You in charge here?"

The angel turned, startled. "Who, me?" His eyelids lowered modestly. "Heavens, no."

"Who is?!" Poppa demanded gruffly. If Poppa had been sent to the Other Place, a question like this in a tone like that would have earned him a quick jab with a red-hot pitchfork. But this was Heaven, where no voice was ever raised in anything but the praise of God, and where no lower angel possessed a scrap of impatience. This mortal creature couldn't know that yet, of course, thought the angel softly. It took a little getting used to, did bliss.

"Well, the Arch Angel is in charge, of course," he said quietly, "but—"

Poppa didn't have time for any "buts." "Where is he??!"

The harried-looking angel with the printout thought for a moment, obviously debating with himself. But one doesn't Refuse, here, of course. Everything is Given.

"He's over there. But I really wouldn't bother him right now. He's not in a very good mood."

He's not in a good mood? What about *me*? Without hesitation, Poppa darted out of the line, to the flabbergasted stares of the other standees and a "Well!" from the lady in curlers. He hurried over (and it felt very strange, walking quickly on nothing but cloud) to where the Arch Angel was standing with several other angels. As he approached, Poppa realized that an argument was going on, although a very quiet one, something like a shouting match in a public library, carried on in whispers.

"He's your responsibility!" the Arch Angel was saying sternly just as Poppa came within earshot.

The angel to whom this reproof was addressed was suddenly very busy folding a pleat in his robe.

"Yes, but he's been doing it for over two hundred years, and—"

"He was acting strange," insisted the Arch Angel. "I saw it. You never should have sent him down. . . ."

"Excuse me," interrupted Poppa, "but I've got to talk to you. . . ."

The Arch Angel turned. He was a tall, imposing being in an immaculate white robe that although as unornamented as the other angel's, it was of a far finer material. It absolutely shimmered. Looking at this mortal with slight impatience, he told Poppa brusquely, "You're supposed to stay in line."

But Poppa wasn't having any of it. "Listen," he said quickly. "I'm not ready for that. I don't want a whole lot of time. Just a few more days."

With a large, commanding hand, the Arch Angel made a gesture of dismissal. "If you're here, *He* called. And there's nothing I can do." Every day it was the same story. At least one of them wasn't ready. At least one of them jumped the line and asked for or begged for or cried for or demanded more time. What was the *matter* with these mortals? Didn't they know this was Heaven, for Heaven's sake? They were the *lucky* ones! Consider the alternative! He turned and strode off like a clipper ship in full sail, with the angel carrying the printout following meekly after him.

Poppa just stood there for a beat, uncertain. This was, after all, Heaven, and for an Irishman like Poppa, it was what he'd prayed for all his life. Not only that, but somewhere inside those gates his darling Mary was waiting for him, just as the priests had promised. Together forever in Paradise. All he had to do was get back in line and, when his turn came up, walk through the gates and he'd get his wings. It was tempting. But no. He shook his head. Some things were more important even than wings. Heaven can wait, he decided. Robbie comes first.

With determination, he charged off after the Arch Angel and caught up with him.

"You don't understand," he puffed, slightly out of breath (which was strange in itself, because hadn't he stopped breathing altogether?). "I made a promise to my grandson, and I've never gone back on my word to him."

The Arch Angel sighed a little. There wasn't an excuse or a reason he hadn't heard millions of times already. Even Shakespeare had asked for a few days more, to write another play. Schubert had pleaded an unfinished symphony. Promises to children were nothing new; they were frequently offered as an excuse for more time.

"Death is an obligation of life," the Arch Angel said matter-of-factly, as if by rote. "He'll come to understand. This is how children learn." Once more, he turned and walked away from Poppa. He had more important business to attend to. Nobody ever got more time. Nobody. Ever.

Yet something in the small mortal's spirit had caught the attention of the meek attendant angel; he stopped and looked back at him curiously before following after his superior.

But Poppa was by no means finished. Mike Halligan had never in his life left a job undone (except the stringing of the Christmas lights, but that's understandable in the circumstances), and he wasn't about to start now. Fired up, he stormed after the boss.

"Let me tell you something," he yelled, and the heavens shook at the unaccustomed roar. "I was a cop in New York for forty-five years, and I saw the city at its worst! But every Christmas something magical happens. There's something in the air! A spirit like nothing else ever anywhere, and I want to show it to my grandson!"

The Arch Angel took a second look at Poppa, and sympathy began to soften his imposing brows. "He's young," he reminded the mortal more gently. "He has plenty of time."

Poppa's shoulders sagged; he was close to being convinced of the hopelessness of his position. He wasn't getting anywhere. "But it's not the same when you're older," he said quietly.

The meek angel was ruffling the pages of his printout as if looking for something. Then he tugged at the sleeve of the Arch Angel's robe. "Sir, may I have a word with you?" he whispered anxiously. The Arch Angel allowed himself to be pulled to one side.

"Please wait right here," said the meek angel to Poppa in an encouraging tone of voice. Mystified, Mike watched the two angels whispering together, glancing at him from time to time. What was going on?

"Did you listen to what he said?" the meek angel was whispering.

"Yes. So what?" Now the Arch Angel was becoming impatient again. They were in the middle of a crisis here, and he had little time to spend on the wishes of mortals.

Holding up the computer printout, the meek angel spoke hurriedly, trying to get it all said before he was interrupted.

"He was a policeman, in New York City." He pointed to a page in the printout. "And it says here he was not *just* a policeman, but a *detective*."

"What are you getting at?" demanded his boss impatiently.

"Didn't you hear how much he loves Christmas in New York?"

"Yes, but—"

The meek angel dared to interrupt, a first. He didn't whisper, but he pitched his voice as low as it would go and gave each word an equal emphasis, to underline their importance. *"I don't think his arrival was an accident,"* he said slowly. "I think *He* sent him...to solve our problems." At the word *He*, he rolled his eyes upward, in the direction of the Throne.

Instinctively (for angels have instincts, too), the Arch Angel also looked up. Then he stared at the attendant angel, over at Poppa, back to the printout, and at Poppa once more as he digested what the lesser angel had told him. Could it be possible?

Poppa stood watching the two angels. They were obviously discussing him, because they both kept glancing in his direction. Also, it seemed to have something to do with the printout. Could there be a chance? Was it possible that...?

Meanwhile, the line had been moving steadily and was growing shorter as the mortals checked through the Pearly Gates into Heaven itself.

"Pssst! Psssst!"

Poppa turned. The octogenarian in the wrinkled hospital gown was making noises at him through toothless gums. "Come on! Come on! Get back in line! You've got to go through the gate!" He pointed to the jogger, who was just passing through in his sneakers. Next in line was the lady in curlers, then the old man, then it would be Poppa's turn.

But Poppa just shook his head. He had no intention of passing St. Peter's Gate unless St. Peter himself kicked him through it. Besides, it looked now as though the two angels had ended their discussion and were in agreement about something, because both of them were nodding and smiling. Sure enough, they were approaching Poppa, and the Arch Angel was saying in a very different tone of voice, "Well, I think we might be able to make a deal."

Heaven or not, angel or no, Mike Halligan had been on the beat too long not to be suspicious of that word.

"A deal?" He frowned.

The Arch Angel nodded, and his face was serious.

"I need help. It seems that *we*"—and here he threw a stern, significant look at the lesser angel—"lost one of our angels."

"He's disappeared in New York City," the other angel hastened to explain. "Using the mortal name of Wiley Boggs, he was sent down to spread the Christmas cheer, something he does every year, a pretty routine assignment, in fact—"

"But he hasn't been heard from since," the Arch Angel finished, his brows contracted in a frown.

The lesser angel nodded sadly. "And we've been getting all kinds of reports, terrible reports. Because of his disappearance, the city is missing its traditional Christmas spirit."

Poppa's eyes widened in disbelief. New York City?

At Christmas? Without Christmas spirit? He couldn't even begin to comprehend it, but now the Arch Angel was speaking again, and Poppa mustered all his attention to listen.

"I may be going out on a limb," the boss angel was saying, "but perhaps your arrival at this time wasn't an accident."

Now it was Poppa's turn to frown. "I don't understand."

As the last of the line was whisked through the Gate, the Arch Angel put his arm around the small man's shoulder and led him off into the clouds. Behind them the Gate clanged shut. Business was over for the day.

"Let me explain," said the Arch Angel. "Now, you're a police detective, right? I mean, you *were* a police detective, right? Well, here's the deal...."

"THE POLICE ARE ON THEIR WAY, AND THE FAMILY DOCtor has been notified," said the older paramedic, putting the phone down. Kate just nodded numbly, her eyes red with weeping, the lids sore. Beside her on the living room sofa, Missy was still sniffling loudly. Robbie, a bundle of pain, was brushing away the tears that insisted on creeping down his cheeks. It had all been over so quickly that the three of them were still in shock.

"Kate!" Rick Westin burst in through the door; they'd called him at his office. He pulled his wife up into his arms, and she buried her head in his shirt front and started to cry again.

"Kate, I'm sorry," whispered her husband, hugging her and stroking her tousled hair.

"It was so sudden," sobbed Kate. "So sudden. I can't believe he's gone. . . ."

A loud crash made everybody jump.

"What was that?" cried Robbie. It sounded like it had come from Poppa's room.

Everybody turned, and a gasp of disbelief went up from every throat. They all stood frozen as Mike Halligan came tearing out of the doorway to his room.

"Where's my brown valise?" he demanded. "We've got to get going!"

"Poppa! Oh, Poppa!" And Robbie launched himself off the sofa and into his grandfather's arms. "You're alive!" Now the tears were streaming down his little cheeks like rain, but they were tears of happiness.

All hell broke loose, with everybody trying to talk at once. Kate and Robbie just hugged the old man, Missy circled around, trying to find room to squeeze into the hug, and the paramedics, caught off-base, were giving each other dirty looks.

"You said he had no pulse, no heartbeat," said the older one to the younger one accusingly.

"He *didn't*," insisted the other. "You were *dead*." He pointed at Poppa.

"Dead? Do I look dead?" In fact, Halligan was looking better than he had in years. There was a brightness to his eyes and a bounce to his step that were the mark of a much younger man.

"I'd better check the equipment," conceded the younger paramedic. "It's fouled up before."

Kate gave her father another squeeze. "Oh, Dad," she murmured. She was so happy that she couldn't find the words. It was a miracle, nothing short of a miracle.

Only Rick Westin tried to remain calm. Somebody had to. "Will someone tell me please what's going on around here?" But nobody was listening. His wife and children were still taking turns squeezing the new life out of Poppa, and the paramedics, shamefaced, were packing up their so-called life-saving gear. The younger one still kept shooting looks at Poppa and muttering to himself, "He was *dead*. He *was* dead."

But Poppa had had enough of jubilation. It was time to get down to business. A deal was a deal. He squirmed his way out of the hug and barked an order to Robbie.

"Go pack! We're going to get an earlier flight. And take plenty of warm clothes!"

Robbie turned eagerly to run to his room, but his father called after him. "Robbie! Come back here! You're not going anywhere until I find out what's going on!"

Reluctantly, Robbie came back into the living room.

"Missy, you got my brown valise?" asked Poppa.

"We'd better get him back in bed," said the older, more experienced paramedic. Dead or alive, this old guy had been through some ordeal, and he needed rest, not an airplane trip lasting six hours.

Kate nodded in agreement and took hold of her father's elbow. "Dad, come on," she urged him gently.

But Poppa pulled away from her. "No, I can't!" he protested.

"You almost died," said Kate, and reached for his hand again.

"Almost?" Poppa's snub-nosed face lit up triumphantly. "Almost? I *did* die. But now I'm back! *On a mission from Heaven!"*

Another gasp went up. "Oh, my God," breathed Kate softly, her face white. It must have been a stroke of some kind, and now Dad's mind was . . . was . . . She couldn't bring herself to even think the word.

"I told you he's been getting senile," said Rick to Kate in an undertone.

"Senile!" roared Poppa, his face red with indignation. "Who's senile? I tell you I died and went up to Heaven, and there were these two angels, see, but I wouldn't go through the Gate, because I have to take Robbie to New York City. And then they said they'd lost an angel, and they made this deal with me, and so here I am!" The speech had left him out of breath, but nobody except Robbie had paid attention to it, over the hubbub that resulted from Poppa's announcement that he'd died and come back. Nobody was interested in the story, only in arguing about what to do with Poppa.

Rick, of course, wanted to shove Poppa smack into the nearest hospital with a geriatrics ward, and the paramedics joined in with their two cents, backing Rick, but Kate put her foot down. Rest is all he needed, insisted Kate. They'd put Dad to bed.

Recognizing a no-win situation when he saw one, Poppa shut his mouth and allowed himself to be led off to bed like a baby. He knew that he'd said too much; how could he expect others to believe such a cockamamie story when he scarcely believed it himself? Now that he was back in the San Fernando Valley, with all its Christmas humidity, Heaven seemed no more than a dream.

But deep inside, Poppa knew that it had been no dream but something very real, and that he'd made a deal and given his word and that he couldn't go back on it. A deal is a deal, isn't it? Especially when you make it with an angel.

THREE

IT WAS LATE, AND THE HOUSE WAS QUIET. Behind her closed bedroom door, Missy slept an exhausted sleep, worn out by the emotions of the afternoon. In the living room, Kate and Rick kept up their ongoing argument in low voices, Rick on the attack, Kate on the defense. They'd been at it for hours and were getting nowhere.

In his room, Robbie lay wide-awake, staring up at the dark ceiling. Moonlight came in through the window and attached itself to the wall opposite Robbie's bed, and he could look at the Reggie Jackson poster and the Lakers pennant on his wall, but he chose instead to look up into the darkness.

He had a lot to think about, and he didn't want distractions.

When his door opened very silently and a smallish figure stole across the room, Robbie didn't jump. He wasn't startled, or even surprised; he'd been expecting it. The figure came close to the bed.

"Hi, Poppa," whispered Robbie.

"Hi, Robbie." Poppa smiled, and in the moonlit room Robbie could see the old man's face quite plainly. Poppa perched on the side of the boy's bed.

"You feelin' okay?" asked Robbie.

"Fit as a fiddle."

"Tell me about the angels again," said Robbie in a very low voice. "I couldn't sleep, thinkin' about what you said."

"You were the only one who believed me," said Poppa warmly.

"You wouldn't lie." The words were spoken simply and were filled with innocent faith.

Poppa gave his grandson an affectionate pat on the shoulder. "No, I wouldn't. And that's why we've got to get going."

Robbie sat up in bed like a shot, and excitement made him squeak. "You mean it?!"

"Shhhhhh." The old man gave an uneasy glance at the door and put one finger to his lips.

Robbie dropped his voice to a whisper. "*I* still get to go?"

Poppa nodded. "That's the only reason I made the deal. Finding that angel will be a snap, and we'll have the rest of the week for ourselves."

Robbie thought this over. "What about Mom and Dad?"

The old man shook his head, and a small, guilty frown creased his forehead. This was the only part he didn't like.

"It's got to be our secret, Robbie."

Robbie was silent for a moment as he turned the ethics of it over in his nine-year-old mind. He was an intelligent boy and, mischief aside, basically a good and honest one. And he knew that this part was the catch and needed resolving.

"Well," he said at last, his head to one side, "if *you* say it's okay, it's got to be. I mean, Mom said you should never argue with your parents, right? And you *are* Mom's father . . . right?"

The two exchanged a grin. Right.

In the living room, the argument continued. It wasn't a new one. To give Rick credit, he wasn't Poppa's enemy. It's just that he was a very conventional man and had grown up in a very conventional home, not far from where he and Kate were living now. In all his life, he'd never encountered anybody as zany and boyish at age sixty-five as his father-in-law, and it made him uncomfortable. It made him doubly uncomfortable that his only son, at the impressionable age of nine, spent so much time with the old man and appeared to be completely under his influence. And now, with this phony heart attack and this crazy talk of angels and a mission from heaven—well, it was more than time to take some action. Poppa would undoubtedly be happier in a home for people of his age, where he could have some company in his delusions. It never occurred to Rick that sixty-five isn't old and that in only twenty-five years he'd be there himself. It never occurred to Rick to take anything Poppa said seriously. How could he?

The two of them had gone over this ground so many times it had worn into a rut. They were both exhausted, longing for bed, yet still they thrashed it out, trying to get the matter settled once and for all.

"Kate, you're just going to have to face the fact," said Rick for perhaps the fiftieth time. "Your father's getting old."

Kate winced. If there was any fact she wasn't ready to face, it was that her exuberant, happy-go-lucky Irish imp of a father was getting old. Wasn't it bad enough she'd lost her mother so recently? Now it seemed to her that Rick was trying to deprive her of her father, too.

"But he's not certifiable," she protested again for what must have been the fiftieth time. "And I resent your saying that to everyone. He was always a character, doing crazy things."

With a firm shake of his dark head, Rick said, "Kate, this isn't the first time he's done something like that.

I'm telling you, he's senile. All that ranting about Heaven and angels. Come on! We're going to have to deal with the problem."

"There's no problem!" repeated Kate defiantly, sticking out her lower lip in exactly the way her father did when he was being stubborn. Every now and again, the Irish in her had to come out.

"He faked a heart attack!" Rick raised his voice heatedly.

"He did not!" Kate shouted back.

"You heard the doctor! There's nothing physically wrong with him!"

But Kate kept shaking her head. She was as puzzled as Rick was disbelieving, but she knew what she had seen. She remembered Poppa's still face the color and texture of wax, the eyes shrunken in their sockets, the chest that didn't rise or fall. "I was here! I saw what happened! I can't explain it, and neither can the paramedics, but he *didn't* fake it, Rick!"

Rick shrugged and blew out a long *whooosh* of breath. "Well, I'm glad we cancelled their trip to New York. I was never hot on the idea, anyway."

Kate shot him a startled look. "You never said anything!"

"He's got too much influence on Robbie. He believes everything your father says, all those wild cop stories."

"You're exaggerating," retorted Kate impatiently.

"They just have a good time together."

"Some good time," snorted Rick. "Your father's on a mission from Heaven, and Robbie has no more sense than to believe him. . . ."

Inside the house, the argument continued.

Outside, it was a very different story.

The night was quite warm and very still. The bright yellow moon, nearly full, shone with extraordinary clarity, giving more light than an arc lamp. Two figures crept quietly across the lawn to the garage. Considering the temperature, they were dressed most peculiarly. Although neither figure was large, the smaller one was distinctive in a snow parka, a muffler, and a woolen cap. The other, which moved more slowly, wore a sweater jacket (red, though the moonlight painted it black) and a cap of Irish tweed on its head. On its hands were black leather gloves; the other figure wore mittens. Both carried suitcases.

"He's a good influence on Robbie," insisted Kate inside the house.

Outside, the influence and the influencee were stealing the family car. Silently they had opened the garage door, and even more silently Robbie had slipped into the front seat. Poppa turned on the ignition, released the brake, and the boy slipped behind the steering wheel while the old man put his shoulder to the rear end of the station wagon and pushed. The Chevy eased out of the garage and wobbled uncertainly down the driveway. It would have moved with more sureness had Robbie been tall enough to see over the wheel. As it was, it was headed straight for a row of galvanized and very noisy garbage cans.

"Watch out!" whispered Poppa sharply.

Robbie spun the wheel with all his nine-year-old might, missing the cans by a margin of inches. Both grandfather and grandson heaved sighs of nervous relief.

"All right!" whispered Poppa. "Turn!" The car headed for the fence dividing the Westin house from the house next door. "No! The other way!"

Foot by foot, the station wagon rolled into the street, down the block, and around the corner. Nobody inside the house saw or heard it go, and when an engine started up a block away, neither Rick nor Kate paid it any attention.

The drive to LAX Airport was uneventful. That is, no head-on collisions actually took place, and near-misses don't count. Irish Mike Halligan, the Terror of the Freeways, simply drove as he'd always driven when he was a detective with a siren and flashing lights on his unmarked car, and everybody on the road had to get out of his official way in a hurry. That was the only way he knew how to drive, weaving in and out of traffic like a broken-field runner holding the pigskin, cutting off limos, airport buses, cabs, Porsches, and anything else on the road.

"Scotty thinks driving with you is better than any ride

at Disneyland," said Robbie proudly as the Chevy Malibu kicked sand in the face of a $62,000 completely restored classic Lagonda that tried to pass it.

Traffic to the Los Angeles airport is always heavy, but at holiday time, especially Christmas, it's a nightmare of stalled cabs and limos, private cars with angry horns blaring, bumpers locked to bumpers ahead of them; it inches rather than flows. Yet Poppa, on a mission from Heaven and with sublime disregard for everything else on the road, managed to get there in record time. When he came to the winding approaches that led to every terminal, and they were choked with unmoving cars, buses, and cabs, he simply went through the parking lots instead, at forty miles an hour going in the wrong direction, until he screeched into the lot opposite the terminal of their airline. They made their plane with three minutes to spare, while other drivers, staring in disbelief, cursed at them and shook their fists.

The plane was filled, seven across, with people going home for the holidays, but Poppa had managed to wangle a window seat for Robbie, who'd never been on a jet before, and whose eyes were round with wonder and darting everywhere. Takeoff was only twenty minutes late.

Once they were in the air, Robbie glued his freckled nose to the window, watching with mounting excitement as the lights of Los Angeles fell away beneath the wings.

"Poppa, look!" he cried excitedly. "I think I can see

our house down there!" Was there ever a nine-year-old boy or girl who didn't say exactly the same thing if he or she had a window seat?

"You might be right. Could be," said Poppa absent-mindedly. He was already turning his thoughts to the mystery that waited for them in New York.

"You think they found our letter yet?" asked Robbie.

"I don't know. But we'll call home as soon as we land. Let them know we're okay."

Robbie smiled and leaned back in his seat. The old man regarded his grandson fondly. He saw the excitement shining in his eyes, the anticipation that reddened the freckled cheeks, and he thought of how little time he had and how much there was to do. Still, certain things would take precedence once the matter of the missing angel was cleared up and out of the way.

"You know, we have a family tradition," he told Robbie. "Every Christmas your grandma and I used to take your mother for a ride in a horsedrawn carriage down Fifth Avenue. Clippity-clop, clippity-clop. You'll love it. We'll see all the decorations, smell the chestnuts roasting, watch the last-minute shoppers rushing home with their packages, and, if we're really lucky, it might even snow."

Robbie turned an eager face to Poppa. "I've never seen snow. Not in real life," he breathed. Oh, if it would only snow!

Poppa reached over and gave the boy a hug.

From John F. Kennedy Airport in New York City, Poppa dialed the Westin house, and the phone was caught up on the first ring.

"Hello, Dad?" called Kate anxiously. She sounded as though she'd been up all night, which she had.

Poppa and Robbie had both crammed into one telephone booth, sharing the receiver between them so both could hear.

"I hope you're not upset, Kate," said Poppa soothingly. "And I want you to know that everything is all right. Robbie's right here with me, and we're going to catch a cab to the hotel."

Kate tried to hang on to her cool, especially with Rick glaring at her over her shoulder. "Don't," she said firmly. "Rick and I think it would be best for you to turn around, right now, and catch the first flight back."

"Don't be silly. Now, listen, I left your station wagon in Lot C, Aisle..." He turned to Robbie for help.

"Aisle *Nine*," said Robbie proudly.

"Yeah," Poppa turned back to the phone. "Lot C, Aisle Nine."

"We're not worried about the car—" began Kate, but Rick grabbed for the receiver.

"Let *me* talk to him!" he said angrily.

Kate pulled it away, out of her husband's reach. She drew a deep breath, and into the receiver she said as calmly as she could, "Dad, we want you and Robbie to come home. What happened to you yesterday was—"

Poppa wouldn't let her continue. "Never mind what happened yesterday," he interrupted, "because I know you don't believe me—"

It was Kate's turn to interrupt. "It's not that I don't believe you—"

But Rick had had quite enough. "Is he talking about those angels again?" he demanded, and he snatched the phone out of Kate's hand. "Give me that! Listen," he yelled at Poppa, "this has gone far enough! I want you on the next plane back here. . . ."

Robbie could hear his father's anger crackling like static from the receiver, but he couldn't make out the words. He looked at Poppa with a question-mark face, and Poppa placed one hand over the mouthpiece and said to Robbie, "You were right. He's not taking this too well."

His anger boiling over at last and the object of it reachable at the other end of a phone, Rick let all his ire out, becoming more and more furious as he talked. "I can't believe you snuck out like that!" he yelled. "I thought it was settled! The trip was off!"

"Now, calm down, Richard," said Poppa mildly.

"'Calm down'?" raved Rick. "You kidnapped my son! And you're . . . you're . . ." He searched for the right words. "You're a senile old man! You're out of touch with reality! Now, you and Robbie get on the next plane out.

Do you hear me? The next plane! Or I'll... I'll..."

It's not too hard to ignore threats when you're three thousand miles away from the threatener. All Poppa said into the phone was a calm "We'll call you from the hotel tonight, and I hope you'll be in a better mood." Then he hung up the receiver, leaving Rick yelling at empty air.

"I can't believe it," Rick exploded to Kate. "He hung up on me!"

Kate took the receiver out of her husband's hand and placed it gently on the hook. "Well, you shouldn't have shouted at him," she told him reasonably.

Missy, still rubbing the sleep from her eyes, came into the living room. "What's all the noise?" she asked plaintively. "You guys woke me up with your yelling."

Rick turned to Kate, icy. He wasn't yelling now; he was very quiet, which told Kate that he meant business. "You'd better pack. We're going to have to go to New York."

Kate merely nodded and went to get the suitcases down from the closet. Her mind was in turmoil. Could Rick be right? Could this attack, whatever it was, that Dad had suffered have sent him around the bend? Was Dad in full control of his senses? Or was he really a danger to himself and to Robbie? Had she confused his normal eccentricity with something a lot more serious? And the terrifying thought came out of nowhere to grip her until she trembled: Would they ever see either of them again?

Poppa hung up the receiver on his yelling son-in-law with a sigh. *I guess I couldn't have expected a different reaction*, he thought. He turned to his grandson.

"I don't want *you* to ever hang up on your father like that," he told the boy, conscious that he had set a bad example. "Understand?"

Robbie nodded.

But Poppa couldn't resist a last lick. "Now, *I* can do something like that, 'cause I'm older, and"—he gave Robbie a big, impish grin—"*senile.*"

THE NIGHT PLANE FROM L.A. HAD GOTTEN INTO JFK about six in the morning, New York time. But by the time Robbie and Poppa had claimed their taxi and had bumped over the pot-holed roads from Queens to Manhattan, it was close to seven-thirty, which is just about when morning arrives in late December, when the days are at their shortest.

So Robbie caught his first glimpse of the skyscrapers of east Manhattan in the thin gray light of dawn, and it was overwhelming. The tops of the buildings picked up the early light, some of them reflecting it with their glass, while others shone like pure gold. It *was* gold, said Poppa. Alloyed gold, maybe, and maybe the thinnest possible coat of it, but gold nonetheless. Gold on the roofs of the city.

As they drove across the 59th Street bridge, Robbie sat open-mouthed, totally awed. Nothing that Poppa had

told him about this city—and he'd told him plenty—
had prepared the boy for his first sight of the Big Apple.
Even in the feeble light of a wintry dawn, it was mag-
nificent beyond description.

But Poppa wasn't awed; his entire small body shook
with excitement and anticipation as he arrived in the city
he loved so much, the city that had borne him and bred
him.

Rolling down the cab window, Poppa stuck out his
head and yelled, "Here we are! Merry Christmas, New
York!!"

Up to now, the cabbie had sat, silent and surly, behind
the wheel, without so much as a greeting. His face was
heavily bandaged, and around the bandages you could
see black and blue bruises. But when Poppa yelled a
greeting to New York, he twisted around in his seat and
asked over his shoulder and with a smirk, "Where'd *you*
fly in from?"

"L.A.," answered Robbie eagerly.

"Got a brother-in-law out there," said the cabbie.
"That's where I'd like to be for the holidays."

Poppa gave his head a vehement shake. "Naaah. New
York's the only place to celebrate Christmas!"

The taxi driver nodded grudgingly. "Usually, yeah,
but not *this* year. Look at *me!*" He pointed to his battered
face, and the cab swerved dangerously, nearly hitting a
Mazda in the next lane. "Got beat up! An' just because

I went out of my way to help somebody!" The driver
shook his head, marveling at his own stupidity in trying
to be a good person. "Well, no more! I can be just as
miserable and mean as the rest of 'em."

Poppa and Robbie exchanged significant glances.

"Boy, *he* sure hasn't got the Christmas spirit."

Poppa nodded, his face serious. "And if everybody is
like him . . . the Arch Angel was right."

"Then you've just got to find that missing angel!"

At the word "angel," the cabbie jolted upright in his
seat and began to eavesdrop harder.

"They were smart sending *me* down," said Poppa.
"They knew I was a good detective and New York was
my beat." He leaned closer to his grandson and dropped
his voice.

"My death was no accident, Robbie." Pointing upward
with his thumb, he added, "*He* needed me."

Two pedestrians had to jump for their lives as the
cabbie, craning his neck back as far as he could to hear
what they were saying, let the cab drive itself.

A question, a serious one, had been in Robbie's mind
for hours and on the tip of his tongue again and again.
Now he asked it, afraid to hear the answer.

"What happens after you find him, Poppa? Do you
have to go back to Heaven?" His blue eyes searched his
grandfather's eyes anxiously.

Poppa looked deeply into his grandson's beloved little

face. Then he nodded. "A deal's a deal," he reminded Robbie gently. "The Arch Angel only gave me until Christmas."

When he saw Robbie's face begin to crumple and tears come into the boy's eyes, he reached out and gave him a loving pat of reassurance. "Hey, Heaven's not a bad place. . . . And I'll get to see your grandmother again." The thought of his darling Mary made Mike smile, and Robbie did his best to smile back.

By now, the cabbie couldn't contain himself a second longer. "'Heaven'?" he haw-hawed. "Thought you said you was from L.A.!" He turned all the way around in his seat, laughing his head off. "I had a fare last week who told me he just got in from Mars!"

His raucous laughing was cut off short by an ear-splitting crash and the sound of metal crunching and glass breaking. Left to its own devices, the taxi had rear-ended a police car parked on 63rd near Madison Avenue. With a jolt that sent everybody flying, the cab came to a halt, its front grille locked firmly in the blue-and-white's rear bumper. Two officers, unhurt but seething with rage, piled out of their car and headed for the terrified cabbie.

"You okay?" Poppa asked Robbie. "Anything broken?"

"No, I'm fine."

The two of them emerged shakily from the rear seat. The impact had made the taxi's trunk fly open, and Poppa took their two suitcases out. Then, with one eye on the meter, which was still running, he reached into his wallet and took out a bill for the cab.

"Here," he said to the driver, who was wincing under the cops' tongue-lashing, "keep the change. We'll walk from here."

It was a winter day in New York, and Robbie had never experienced one. Even though Poppa had seen to it that the boy was warmly dressed, the cold seemed to get in everywhere, and Robbie shivered. His nose was a piece of ice, and the fingers in his mittens ached with the cold. Even though his knitted cap was pulled down over his ears, he felt a tingling in his lobes. It was cold! And windy, too. Robbie saw pieces of newspaper and fast-food wrappers being blown around the streets by the wind, attaching themselves to people's legs. *Why can't they pick them up and throw them in the litter bins that stand on every corner?* wondered Robbie. *Poppa didn't tell me that New York was so dirty.*

And the people! Even in this bitter cold, they were everywhere, scurrying through the gray streets on their way to work, faces averted from one another, no word of greeting on their lips. Robbie thought he'd never seen so many people all in one place, or such unhappy ones, either. Even though they didn't seem to want to touch one another, still they managed with an elbow or a shoulder to push others out of their way.

Boy, if this is New York City, I don't think I'm going to like it, thought Robbie. *Not even with carriage rides or skating at Rockefeller Center.* He trudged after Poppa.

Cindy Mills adjusted her Channel Three microphone and tested it; it was live. She nodded to her cameraman and waited for the signal that tape was rolling. Mikes were often a problem in cold or hot weather; they were sensitive to extremes of temperature. And on a day like today, you couldn't wear a body mike outdoors, because sound might be muffled by heavy winter clothing. Cindy shivered and pulled her sheepskin collar higher up around her neck. Down here at City Hall it was practically sub-Arctic! The tall municipal buildings around the park plaza created wind tunnels, and the icy blasts came whistling through them, across City Hall Park, and up the steps, heading straight for Cindy.

All around her, city legislators, their faces angry and disgruntled, were pushing their way out of the revolving doors and jostling one another down the steps. Their eyes looked tired and disappointed. And there was an air of sullenness about them that was at variance with the season.

Cindy waited until the jostling was over and the legislators had stepped into the limos or cars or had gone off yelling for taxicabs. She was a fine-looking small young woman in her late twenties, with good legs and a beautiful pair of eyes, good teeth, thick, dark hair cut short in a gamine bob, and all the other plusses that television executives look for in on-camera personalities. But she was more than that. Cindy was a newsperson, and the city was her beat. She loved the feeling of her fingers on New York's pulse; she loved digging out interesting features about the city and putting them on the air.

That is, she loved putting *certain* stories on the air, but not all of them. Not this one. This story she hated, and she hated being the one to bring it to Mr. and Mrs. New Yorker.

But Cindy was nothing if not a professional, so when the "tape-rolling" signal came from her cameraman, she stepped forward with her microphone and looked straight into the videocam lens. Then she delivered her story.

"Bah, humbug. That seems to be the new motto of City Hall. Over the last several weeks, the Council has passed a series of controversial resolutions that most members admit are but token gestures to cut back expenses in our near-bankrupt city. First, they vetoed the necessary funds for police support, thus forcing the cancellation of the traditional Pre-Christmas Parade. Then, in the name of energy conservation, they banned the traditional Christmas lights and decorations. And finally, less than five minutes ago, the City Council passed Resolution 356, which will withdraw all city contributions to the traditional Christmas Day charities." Now her detachment left her, and Cindy's own feelings became evident.

"So much for tradition and charity." Her voice echoed her disappointment. "The parade's gone and the lights are out. Thanks to the City Council, it's shaping up to be a very dim Christmas. This is Cindy Mills reporting from City Hall."

Solemnly, she looked long enough into the camera for the tape to stop rolling, then she told her minicam man "That's a cut," by making a fake slash at her own throat.

"That's it, Jim. Let's get the tape back to the station." Disconnecting her mike, Cindy helped Jim load the bulky equipment into the Channel Three van, but she wasn't her customary cheerful, chatty self. Her usually merry face was sad and troubled.

By the time they reached their hotel, Robbie was almost frozen stiff, but the hotel lobby was very warm— overheated, in fact—with steam rattling noisily through the pipes in cheerful defiance of the City Council's Save-Energy ordinance. Robbie felt the blood coming back to his mittened fingers and booted toes.

The Mayflower hotel stood on Central Park West, just a few blocks north of midtown. It had a continental charm, and was kept in immaculate condition, although it no longer had the elegance and high gloss of the more expensive high-rise hotels downtown. But to Robbie's nine-year-old eyes, it was wonderful—the Helmsley Plaza and the Waldorf all rolled into one.

"Here we are," said Poppa enthusiastically. "Ritzy, huh? Your grandmother and I used to come here for dinner on our anniversaries."

The old man and the boy exchanged smiles, Robbie's expectant, Poppa's nostalgic.

A middle-aged bellman, old far beyond his years, was shuffling toward them dourly, eyeing the pair with mingled disdain and suspicion.

"You want me to take those?" He pointed to the two suitcases.

"Sure," nodded Poppa, handing the bags over. He reached into his wallet and extracted two singles, putting them into the bellman's hand. "Thanks."

The bellman made no move to pocket the tip, but stood looking at the crumpled bills in his hand. Poppa began to bristle.

"Whatssamatter? Not enough?"

The other man shook his head. "No, no . . . it's fine. It's just that you're the first one to tip me all morning." He picked the bags up and headed toward the front desk with them, with Poppa and Robbie following.

They decided to register, get a bite to eat, and see what would happen next. Robbie was beginning to feel very excited. Not only was he here in New York City with his grandfather, but he was about to see the great Mike Halligan, detective, go to work. And they would be tracking not a missing person but a missing angel!

FOUR

THE CHANNEL THREE NEWSROOM WAS JUMP-
ing. Phones kept ringing and were left to ring un-
answered; typewriters clacked; wire services spat
out news stories from glass-domed machines; desk-
top computer terminals glowed, their green screens
covered with words, words, words. There were
fewer than three hours until the midday news, which
went on mostly live, was to go on the air. The art
department was assembling the visuals that would
back any story that didn't have film, minicams
were still out all over the city, and editors were
checking what the satellites were bringing in from
abroad, looking for lead stories.

Mel Shanuck, the station manager, was in his usual pre-broadcast sweat. Mel sweated before the seven A.M. news, before the twelve noon news, and before the six o'clock news. A good thing he wasn't responsible for the eleven o'clock news, or he wouldn't have a drop of moisture left in his burly body. Tie loose, shirt sleeves rolled above his elbows, Mel was ruffling through the papers on his clipboards, reordering his priorities for the fifteenth time that day. All around him, assistants and interns rushed to do his bidding.

Looking up from his board, he saw Cindy Mills threading her way through the maze of the newsroom, and he pounced.

"You got the City Council tape? I want to run it at noon."

Cindy nodded without enthusiasm and handed the cassette over.

"Heard they passed 356," said Mel.

The girl shrugged, and her face darkened. "What did you expect?"

One of Mel's eyebrows went up to his hairline. "A little show of seasonal cheer. What's gotten into those damn people on the council? How much money could they have saved the city? Petty cash!"

"It's a gesture," said Cindy. "Something they hope will be seen in Washington. Maybe they *think* it'll help push through another Federal bailout...." She shrugged again, and shook her head. "Dumb, dumb, dumb."

Together they walked down the corridor to the editing room, where Mel handed the videotape over to a technician.

"We're gonna run this on the newsbreak," he informed the man. "Tell Steve." Then he took Cindy by the elbow.

"Now you've got to get me something for tomorrow night. The Christmas Eve broadcast."

Cindy's expression didn't change. "Like?" she asked wearily.

"Human interest. Upbeat, please."

"Easier said than done," Cindy sighed. Upbeat. She hadn't seen anything upbeat since Halloween, when an acrobat dressed as a pumpkin tried to climb the World Trade Center.

ROBBIE COULDN'T GET OVER THE TALL BUILDINGS. EACH skyscraper appeared to him to be taller than the one before. A whole army of them stretched down Sixth Avenue from Central Park South, tall structures of glass and steel, with clouds reflected in their windows.

"Which one is the Empire State Building?" he asked his grandfather, craning his neck to look up to the roof of the building they were passing.

"It's down on Thirty-fourth Street," Poppa replied. "Don't worry. I'm going to show you everything. But first we've got to run by my old precinct, to see if we can get a lead on the missing angel. All we know is what the Arch Angel told me. He's short, fat, and using the mortal name of Wiley Boggs."

Half a block ahead of them, a crowd had gathered on the sidewalk.

"What's going on there?" asked Robbie, pointing.

Poppa gave him a proud smile. "Oh, that's Rumplemayer's. They're famous for their window display every Christmas."

But when they reached the famous candy store, they were surprised to hear the crowd jeering and booing. What was going on? The crowd kept yelling, as though taking sides.

"Leave her alone!" "Pick on someone your own size!" "Bite her, shorty, bite her."

Poppa bent over and hoisted Robbie up onto his shoulders so that he could see over the crowd. The boy took a good look and gasped.

The window had been gorgeously decorated and bore a sign that said "Kris Kringle's Kitchen." The kitchen was right out of a storybook, with pine furniture and a black iron stove, and cheerful pictures on the wall. But what was happening in the window was not so cheerful a picture.

There were real people in the window, not costumed mechanical figures. Some little men were dressed as elves, and there was a stout, jolly-looking lady in a white wig and an apron as Mrs. Kringle, but the fight they were having was humongous. The famous Rumplemayer confectionery, most of it chocolate and gooey, was everywhere—the elves were flinging it around the kitchen at one another, along with tiny pies, in what was a serious and rather vicious food fight. Mrs. Kringle kept attempting to interfere, to bring peace to the kitchen and the window, but she wasn't having much success. Her white apron and red dress were covered in splashes of chocolate, and she had fudge clinging to the bun of her wig. Every now and again, one of the elves would aim at her instead of at another elf.

"Can you see what's going on?" asked Poppa.

"There's three elves," reported a wide-eyed Robbie. "They're having a food fight, and Santa's wife is trying to stop them!"

"What?" Poppa couldn't believe his ears. In Rumplemayer's window? Impossible!

Now the store manager was on the scene, coming into the window through the back curtain. As soon as they saw him, the elves opened fire, making him the new target for the sticky pies. Wham! And wham! Another bull's-eye! The crowd of spectators went bananas.

"Give it to him!" they encouraged the elves gleefully. "Let him have it!"

Robbie leaned down to tell Poppa in his ear, because the spectators were making so much noise.

"Now some man's in the window! And they're smacking him with pies!"

Poppa had to see this for himself. His beloved Rumplemayer's the scene of a manic food fight, like some demented Three Stooges movie? Not even if he saw it with his own eyes!

But it was true, as Poppa found out when he'd pushed and shoved his way into the jeering, yelling crowd and came close enough to the window to see the three midgets pelting the manager and the stout lady with everything they could get their hands on. Pies, candy canes, lollipops for good little boys and girls—all went hurtling through the air, and many of them hit their target. The window was a shambles and was fast becoming a massacre.

For the first time, Poppa experienced full realization of the job he had on his hands. When Christmas spirit is missing in an entire city, what moves in to take its place? The opposite, of course. And what was the opposite of the Christmas spirit? Meanness and malice, the desire to hurt somebody, anybody. This was terrible! Here was his beloved city in the grip of bad feelings, no peace on earth, bad will toward humankind.

"Something's really wrong in this town," breathed Poppa, upset and miserable.

"I bet if Mom and Dad could see what's going on, they'd believe your story," Robbie told him.

"Come on, son. We have to get moving. We've got

work to do. We gotta find that angel double-quick, before
things really get out of hand!"

The two of them fought their way through the crowd
and came up breathless on the corner. Then they turned
south from 59th Street, heading for the stationhouse.
They didn't even notice the Channel Three camera van
that was cruising the streets, looking for Cindy Mills's
"upbeat story."

"There's a crowd," called Cindy. "Let's stop here and
see what's going on. Might be a story in it. Pull over."

Jim stopped on the corner and shouldered his minicam
as the two of them got out. They were just in time to
see the "elves" dashing out of the side door of Rumpelmayer's, followed by an angry man wearing what seemed
to be a chocolate suit. Puffing after them was a heavy
lady with a white wig half-on, half-off her head, and
smudges of whipped cream all over her face.

"Come back with those costumes!" yelled the furious
manager.

Cindy looked at Jim and Jim looked at Cindy. What
the hell was going on in this city?

ROBBIE HAD NEVER BEEN IN A POLICE STATION BEFORE.
And of all the police stations in the world, Midtown was
one of the busiest. It covered New York from 34th Street
to 57th Street, from the Hudson to the East River, and
maybe three million people lived or worked in its juris-

diction. This was no pussycat-up-a-tree precinct; it dealt with homicides; muggers, bank robbers, arsonists, and worse, every hour of every day. Twenty-four hours, seven days a week. Robbie had heard a hundred hair-raising stories from Poppa about this precinct house, but nothing had prepared him for the thrill of actually being here and seeing it himself.

It was an old building, bearing the scars of time and usage. Eight stories of stone, two green lights burning outside, blue-and-whites parked outside, and unmarked vehicles—mostly Dodges—parked and double-parked up and down the street. They went up the front steps. The floors were of ancient tile, and an ugly green paint was peeling from the walls. The lighting made everybody look as green as the room. Against one wall stood a high desk with three telephones on it. Behind it sat the desk sergeant on duty, eyes watchful. Poppa gave him a familiar wave as he led Robbie to an ancient elevator.

The detective squad room was on the third floor, and it wasn't any better-looking than the downstairs—worse, in fact. A heavy haze of cigaret smoke hung in the air, even though the room was large. Full ashtrays sat on every desk, and it smelled as if the windows had not been opened since they'd been installed, back in 1932. Although the room was large, it was nevertheless crowded. At least ten old wooden desks were scattered around, with chairs drawn up in front of them and other chairs next to them. Heavy steel filing cabinets lined two walls of the room. The telephones rang constantly, but unlike the phones in the TV newsroom, these were picked up promptly. Each phone call represented an emergency, a possibly life-threatening situation.

Detectives of various ages and races were sitting at most of the desks, and many of the chairs were filled by citizens filing complaints or reporting crimes. Busy and noisy, the room reverberated with energy and life, and Poppa took a deep, happy, nostalgic breath of the stale, smoky air. Ahhh! This was more like it! This was home!

"Which was your desk, Poppa?" asked Robbie.

Mike grinned his Irish grin as he proudly led his grandson over to a desk against one wall. It was piled high with a clutter of papers, but it was unoccupied.

"Here it is!"

At the sound of a voice, the detective at the next desk looked up from the report he was taking from a fearful-faced old man. He squinted across at Poppa, as though he couldn't quite make him out.

"Halligan?"

Poppa turned. "Jimmy!"

Jimmy Ramos interrupted his interrogation and rose to walk over and take Poppa's hand.

"I thought it was you!"

Poppa put a hand on Robbie's shoulder, urging him forward. "This is my grandson, Robbie. I brought him to New York to show him a *real* Christmas. Out on the Coast, they've got pink trees and don't know what it's all about."

Robbie gave the detective a shy smile, which the man returned. "Well, welcome back," said Ramos. "It's great to see you, Mike." To the boy, he said, "You know, your grandpa was the best detective in the precinct." At the boy's proud nod, he continued. "He broke me in. He taught me everything." Ramos glanced across at his own desk, where his witness was looking more nervous than ever. It was time to get back to work.

"Hey, stick around," he said to Poppa. "As soon as I take this report, we can talk."

But Poppa was pressed for time. This might not be as easy as he'd thought, putting a whole city back together again.

"Where's the captain?"

"On his way back," called Ramos over his shoulder. "He'll be here any minute."

Poppa pulled the ancient oak swivel chair out from behind his old desk and settled into it. As he leaned back, it made a loud protesting squeak.

"Same old squeak." Mike grinned.

But Robbie was remembering Poppa's stories, and now he was looking hard at the large, cluttered bulletin board.

"Hey, where's the bullet hole?" he demanded.

"Huh?" Then Poppa, too, remembered. He spun around in his chair and pointed to the upper corner of the wooden frame. "Up there. See it?"

Robbie walked right up to the board and studied the frame for a minute. The upper left corner bore a large scarred dent, unmistakably a hole.

"Yeah," the boy breathed, fascinated.

"Only missed my head by inches." Poppa shook his head as he recalled the terrifying episode. "Crazy man. Wasn't out of the pen more'n a couple o' hours. He wanted revenge, 'cause I sent him up."

Robbie gave a delighted shiver at the thought of it, and his skinny little arms broke out in goosebumps.

At this moment, the squad room door opened, and a tall, muscular man whom nobody could ever take for anything but a cop came charging through it, already barking orders. It was Captain Santini, a thirty-year veteran of the force, and a man who saw more of life in a month than many others did in a lifetime.

"Simpson!" yelled Santini. "They need you down in Forensics! Ramos! Did Henderson call from Central?"

"Nope!" called Jimmy.

"All right!" the captain barked back. "Then someone's gotta go down there." He looked around the room to make the assignment. Every detective was tied up except Halligan, who was leaning back in that squeaky old chair of his, grinning at the captain like a happy monkey.

"Halligan! Get down there, and—" Stopping in his tracks, Santini did a double take. "Mike!" he exploded, crossing the room. "What are you doing here?"

"Looking for someone," said Poppa seriously. "And I haven't got much time."

Santini just nodded; a busy cop doesn't waste words. He led Poppa over to something the old man hadn't noticed before. In a corner of the old squad room was a computer desk, with a terminal, keyboard, and printer. It gleamed in sharp contrast to the shabbiness of its surroundings.

"All I've got is a name and a general description," Poppa told the captain.

"Give me the name."

"Wiley Boggs."

The captain sat down at the keyboard and pressed the POWER ON button. At once, the screen glowed into life.

Using two fingers in a hunt-and-peck, Santini punched the name into the data bank, asking for information.

"Let's see if we've got anything. B-O-G-G-S comma W-I-L-E-Y. Right?"

Poppa nodded as he stared at the computer.

"When did you get that thing?"

"Right after you left," Santini grunted. "It works, but I hate it." Words were appearing, flashing across the screen.

"Looks like we've got something." The captain leaned

forward to read. "Boggs, Wiley. Arrested twelve twenty-two. . . ."

"Yesterday," said Robbie, getting excited.

"D and D . . ." read the captain.

"Drunk and disorderly," Poppa informed Robbie.

More words were appearing on the green glowing screen.

"No known address," read Santini. "No priors. Transferred to Bellevue for observation. . . ."

Suddenly, Ramos stood up in his chair, recalling the incident. "You remember!" he shouted across the room at Santini. "That was the nut who kept screamin' he was an angel!"

"Oh, yeah!" said Santini, too intent on the computer screen to notice that Mike and Robbie had exchanged triumphant glances. The angel! They had him! They knew exactly where he was! All they had to do was go to Bellevue and collar him, and that would be it! Case closed!

THE WORD "BELLEVUE" MEANS "BEAUTIFUL TO LOOK upon," and when the building went up in late Victorian times, it probably lived up to its name. But age and the dirt of the city had turned the original red brick into a muddy brown, and the building itself had been added onto over the decades, so now it was a melange of styles—everything from Gothic Revival to Utility Corrugated

Shed. It is a rabbit warren of a city hospital, with inter-connecting corridors and walkways leading from building to building.

And here's an odd thing. Although Bellevue functions as a full-service hospital—with surgeons and dentists and ophthalmologists and pediatricians and podiatrists and gall-bladder specialists—because it also has a large mental ward, the name "Bellevue" has become synon-ymous over the years with "loony bin." "Being taken to Bellevue" never means having a broken leg set; it means you're under psychiatric observation.

It's about a fifteen-minute cab ride from the Midtown precinct to 26th Street and the East River, where Bellevue stands. In holiday traffic, make that an hour and fifteen minutes. While Poppa and Robbie sat behind a ticking taxi meter, impatient to claim their Bingo prize—one angel, Boggs comma Wiley—let's see what was going on across town, in the hallowed halls of Bellevue.

Dr. Ingrid Ullman was finding herself stymied. She saw a good number of delusional patients in her office in her three-times-a-week psychiatric stint at the hospital, but never had she met one who so completely clung to his delusion as this chubby, balding man who sat opposite her claiming to be an angel. The funny thing was that if you were asked to describe him, you might very well call him "angelic," because he bore a great resemblance to cherubs in Renaissance paintings.

But if he *were* an angel, he wasn't a very heavenly one. He seemed to be in a pretty foul temper as he snapped at the doctor, "Why don't you believe I'm an angel?"

Dr. Ullman regarded Mr. Boggs quietly across the expanse of her modern desk. She saw a small, plump man in institutional khakis, who, despite the tranquilizers they had given him on the ward, was as bright-eyed and vinegary as when he had been brought in, although a lot more sober.

She made a note on her pad to change his medication as she told him, "I'd *like* to believe in angels, but reality tells me there are no such things."

"But *whose* reality, doctor?"

No question about it, thought Dr. Ullman. *Schizophrenics are clever*. Aloud, she changed the tack of her questioning.

"Mr. Boggs, if you *are* an angel, what are you doing in New York? Why aren't you in Heaven?"

"I told you. I'm down here on assignment, to spread the Christmas cheer. Oh, yes, I've been doing it a long, long time, and I've always requested New York, because it's fun." But a sad expression crept over the little man's face and he shook his head. "But not this year. People just don't seem to care. It's their attitude . . . rush, rush, rush, push, push, push. Oh, I tried. I really did, but—"

Suddenly, Boggs jumped to his feet. "Listen, doctor. I've got to get out of here. I'm in enough trouble as it is." He rolled his eyes heavenward. "They can't be happy about what's happening down here, and they're going to blame *me*."

Dr. Ullman saw a possible lead here and was quick to take it. "Is that why you got drunk?" she asked him pointedly.

The little man cast his eyes down in shame and slowly nodded his head. "I had no control over the situation," he confessed. "That had never happened before. Yes, so I had a drink. I never had one before. I didn't know what it would do." He raised his eyes to hers candidly, and the doctor thought again, *How ironic that he's so angelic*.

"In the past, how did you control the situation?" she asked him.

"I have powers," began Boggs, then his shoulders drooped and the corners of his mouth turned down. "Or, at least, I *had* them." He looked confused. "I'm not sure now," he admitted.

"What did you do with these powers?"

The corners of Boggs's mouth turned up a fraction.

"I made people feel happy, full of joy."

Dr. Ullman took some more notes on her writing pad. He certainly did believe that he was an angel, a messenger from God, this strange little man. At least his psychosis was harmless, even benevolent. That was rare these days.

But Wiley Boggs was on his feet now, impatient to be out of Dr. Ullman's office. "Doctor, I've got to get going," he told her, edging toward the door.

The psychiatrist put her pen down and stood up.

"Yes, maybe we have had enough for today. I'll take you back to the ward, and we can continue our discussion tomorrow. I'd like to pick up with why you feel the need to make people happy."

They passed through the office door and into the corridor. Because the psychiatric division was a high-security section of the hospital, there were guards in the corridors and the doors to the wards were kept locked at all times. Never were patients allowed to roam the halls unattended as they were in maternity or surgical wards.

Leading the way, Dr. Ullman took a few steps down the hall toward Boggs's ward, then she stopped, realizing that the little man was not following her. He was standing exactly where she'd left him, outside the door to her office.

"Come on, Mr. Boggs. The ward is this way."

But the little man just smiled at her. And such a smile! It was positively beatific; it made Dr. Ullman smile back without thinking twice. Not only that, but a strange light suffused the hospital corridor, a gleaming pearlescence, and it appeared to be emanating from the little man, as though he were cloaked in a radiant aura. At the same time, the most heavenly music, the melody of a thousand harps, seemed to pour like golden honey into Dr. Ullman's ears.

And, the strangest thing of all, she found herself walking *up* the corridor, toward the way out, instead of *down* the corridor, to the ward. And now Mr. Boggs was walking . . . or was he floating? . . . with her.

As they walked (or whatever they were doing) together, Dr. Ullman looked at Mr. Boggs with a puzzled smile on her face.

"Why are we walking this way?"

"Because it's the way *out*," said Wiley Boggs, happy now that his powers were restored.

"Mr. Boggs, I am *not* releasing you."

Yet when the two of them arrived at the locked and barred end of the hallway and the uniformed guard stepped forward, Dr. Ullman found herself—against her will, against her intention, against all medical practice, and against all hospital rules—saying to the guard, "It's all right. I'm releasing this patient."

"You're the doctor." And the uniformed guard pressed the button that opened the electric lock; the barred door slid back, and doctor and patient passed through the gate and into the public hallway.

Why did I do that? I didn't want to do that!

But Dr. Ullman couldn't help herself, and what is more, she couldn't seem to stop smiling. She felt somehow filled with joy and a feeling of extreme well-being.

Inexplicable. Nonscientific.

They arrived at the elevators, and Dr. Ullman, still totally baffled and still smiling, saw that Wiley Boggs got safely on a "down" elevator and accompanied him to the main floor.

Naturally, the next "up" elevator was the one that Mike Halligan and Robbie Westin stepped out of. As soon as the elevator disgorged them onto the psychiatric floor, they looked around for help.

"Let's find somebody who can tell us," said Poppa.

He looked around for a person in authority, and the first one he saw was a nurse walking briskly down the corridor.

"Excuse me, where can I—"

"Information's on the first floor," the nurse said brusquely, without stopping. So much for Florence Nightingale.

Poppa shook his head as he looked after her. Two orderlies were gossiping near the wall, and Poppa approached them.

"Can you guys tell me where—"

But they turned their backs on him and continued to talk only to each other. This was crazy! What was happening to people? He looked at Robbie, Robbie looked at him, and they both shrugged hopelessly.

A tall, handsome man observing them stepped up with a friendly smile on his face. He wore a white medical coat, and a stethoscope was stuffed into one of the pockets.

"You seem to need some help," he ventured.

Poppa turned. "Oh, yeah, thanks." He smiled. "I'd like to see one of the patients."

The doctor regarded them seriously from behind horn-rimmed glasses.

"You know this is a detention ward. Visitors must have police clearance."

Poppa reached into his jacket pocket and pulled his leather badge case out, flipping it open to reveal his gold N.Y.P.D. detective's badge.

The doctor leaned forward and inspected the badge very carefully. "I've never seen one like that before."

Poppa opened his mouth to tell a convincing lie, but he hesitated, flustered. For one thing, he never lied, no matter what the circumstances. It wasn't in his nature. For another, he was on a mission from Heaven, and nobody doing God's business should lie. But perhaps most important of all, Robbie was standing right there looking at his grandfather with such pride. He knew that Poppa never lied, and Poppa wouldn't let Robbie down.

"Ahhh, it's what they give you when you retire," he admitted.

The handsome doctor gave him a piercing look.

"So you're not a policeman anymore?"

"No," confessed Poppa. "But I've got to see a man they're holding here."

"It's really important," added Robbie, giving the doctor a pleading look.

The doctor looked down into Robbie's trusting face. He weighed the pros and cons, his brow furrowed in thought. He bit his lip. He sighed. He drew in a deep breath, and finally he said, "I really shouldn't be doing this.... but come on. I guess we can make an exception."

Joyfully, the two followed him down the corridor.

"I'm Dr. Kent," the man informed him as he led the way. "What's the patient's name?"

"Boggs. Wiley Boggs," said Poppa promptly.

Dr. Kent looked thoughtful. "Ah, yes, Boggs..." he murmured.

Robbie tugged at Poppa's jacket, and when he'd gotten his grandfather's attention, he whispered, "He's the first nice person we've met since we've been in New York."

Poppa nodded his agreement; he was beginning to get back some of his faith in his city. So far, this had been a humiliating experience for him. He'd so wanted to show Robbie a great time, and the city had let him down. Except for the precinct, where they still thought of him as one of their own, Poppa had encountered nothing but the worst side of New York to expose his grandson to—all the dirt, the bad manners, the callous indifference for which New Yorkers are notorious, but which Poppa knew wasn't universally true. This kindly Dr. Kent was restoring Poppa's confidence in New York.

"There he is!" shouted a voice.

Two burly attendants were racing toward them down the corridor. Instantly, "Dr. Kent" went wild! He backed away, eyes rolling, and ripped off his doctor's jacket, flinging it to the floor. The jacket was followed by his shirt. The man was wearing a blue T-shirt with a red and yellow "S" emblazoned on it. Superman? Kent? Oh, no!

As the attendants lunged for him, the escaped psycho leaped up on the nurses' station and attempted to fly. Actually, he wasn't bad at it, managing to evade his keepers as he hit the ground running.

"*In*-sane," breathed Robbie, amazed.

Now the "superhero" had whipped off his horn-rimmed glasses and was waving them around like a sword.

"You fools *never* recognize me with my glasses on!" he yelled triumphantly.

The chase was on as patient and guards, doctors, and attendants raced pell-mell down the corridors, with "Superman" in the lead. Poppa moved quickly to yank Robbie out of harm's way, as the melee came barreling past them. Chairs were overturned, vases of flowers left for patients were smashed, and guards tripped over each other in their antic race to capture one looney. It was pure Marx Brothers.

"Metropolis needs me!" shouted Our Hero, and he leaped through the air, landing on his belly on an un-attended gurney, a rolling stretcher. Propelled forward by the man's weight, the gurney rolled swiftly down the corridor, heading for the elevator bank. As if by magic, one set of elevator doors opened and the gurney rolled in, crashing into the far wall. Guards leaped after it, cornering Superman.

The only passenger in the elevator was Ingrid Ullman, who was just returning to her office, having seen Wiley Boggs safely down to the street and out the front door of Bellevue.

This hoohah broke the spell around her, and she realized for the first time what she had done.

But realizing it herself and explaining it intelligently to the police—or even the ex-police—were two entirely different matters.

Once inside Dr. Ullman's office, Poppa was all business; he'd turned back into a detective. He riffled through Boggs's slender hospital folder, supplied by the hospital's police liaison, coming up with the mug shot taken when the angel had been busted for D & D. It showed a sweet-faced chubby man with very little hair, wearing a number on his chest. The man was sporting a Santa Claus outfit with the cap and beard removed for the photograph. The only other piece of evidence was the Santa suit itself, which had been exchanged for the hospital garments that Boggs was presumably now wearing.

Dr. Ullman was embarrassed by Poppa's questions, and he didn't press her hard. After all, he knew that the shrink had been up against a genuine angel, hardly fair odds.

"I just don't know why I released him," Dr. Ullman mused again, shaking her head. "It just seemed right at the time."

"Maybe he used his angel powers on you," said Robbie sympathetically. But he caught Poppa's eye and saw the brief, stern shake of the old man's head. Mum's the word. "Just kidding," the boy added hastily.

But the psychiatrist wasn't even listening. She stood up from her desk and began to pace around the office, her forehead creased with worry as she tried to figure it out.

"I've never done anything like that before. . . ." She couldn't get over her behavior, and behavioral psychology was her specialty. Supposed to have all the answers, now she was no longer even sure of the questions.

Poppa had finished his examination of the Santa suit, and now he asked, "Is this all he had on him? Nothing in the pockets?"

The woman shook her head, and Poppa gestured for Robbie to come and have a look. The label inside the Santa outfit said, "Renta Santa, N.Y.C." A definite clue.

Picking up the mug shot from the psychiatrist's desk, Poppa stowed it safely away into his jacket pocket.

"At least we know what he looks like. . . ." Stuffing the costume back into its paper bag, he tucked it under his arm to return to the N.Y.P.D. liaison office. ". . . And we've got a lead. Come on," he said to Robbie.

As they closed the door to Dr. Ullman's office behind them, they could still hear the doctor murmuring to herself.

"Why did I do it? Why on earth did I let him go?"

The answer, of course, wasn't to be found on earth at all.

"CAPTAIN!" YELLED RAMOS OVER THE SQUAD ROOM noise. "It's for you! Line forty-three. Long-distance from California!"

Captain Santini picked up the phone and identified himself. A worried female voice came out of the receiver.

"Captain, it's Kate Westin, Mike Halligan's daughter."

"Kate! How are you? Your father just left here. He looks great—"

"He was there?" Kate's interruption held a note of alarm. "Was my son with him?"

"Robbie, yeah. Cute kid," replied the captain. He could almost feel the mother's relief pouring out of the phone.

Kate's white knuckles relaxed their tight grasp on the receiver just a little. Poppa and Robbie were alive and well and had been seen, both of them. That was something to be thankful for!

"Listen, Captain," she continued. "I'm worried about Dad. He's not well. We're not sure if he had a heart attack or what. But he took Robbie without our permission...."

"He *kidnapped* him!" Rick yelled into the phone.

Kate pulled the receiver away. "My husband and I are about to board a plane. We're at the gate now, and we'll be in New York tonight. But if there's anything you can do...I mean, to find Dad and hold him, I'd appreciate it."

"Kate, we'll get on it right away," Santini promised. "I'll talk to you as soon as you get in."

He hung up the phone and sat there for a minute, trying to collect his thoughts. What a screwy business! Mike Halligan—the best damn detective Santini had ever known and the most honest man—Halligan had run off with his own grandchild? Didn't make sense. That didn't sound like Mike. And what had she said about a heart attack?

"Ramos!" roared the captain.

The detective stood up from his desk and came over at the summons. "Yeah?"

"Didn't old Halligan look good to you?"

"Sure did. Like a million bucks before taxes."

Santini shook his head, his lips pursed. Didn't make sense. Then he shrugged. "Do me a favor," he told the detective. "Mike was headed down to Bellevue, looking for that crackpot who called himself an angel. See if you can find him. Make up something...anything...but tell him I've got to see him."

"Sure." Ramos nodded, his face puzzled. "I'll get on it right away. I'll find him."

FIVE

WHATEVER THE REASON WILEY BOGGS THE angel had disappeared, it wasn't to spread the Christmas spirit. That much was still evident by the wrap of gray gloom that still hung over the city. People walked around with scowls on their faces. The department stores, which depend on the annual Christmas rush for most of their income, and which by now would be busting at the seams with last-minute shoppers, were nearly deserted. Thanks to the save-energy ordinance passed by the City Council, the streets were almost dark. The big office buildings were usually decorated with huge twinkling stars and Christmas trees made of thousands of lights, which could be seen from a mile away. Now they were just buildings, nothing more.

Hardly anybody was standing in line to look at the department store windows, and the windows themselves were lackluster, maybe because they knew that nobody was looking at them. Children were not stacked six-deep outside the F.A.O. Schwarz toy store on Fifth Avenue, trying to get a peek at the wonderful goodies in the windows. Every other year, perhaps, but not this one. The sidewalk Santas, ringing their bells for charity, weren't collecting any money; nobody seemed to want to give anything to anybody, not presents, not charity. The chestnut vendors weren't making money either, and they always did phenomenal business at this time of the year, because hot roasted chestnuts and Christmas go so well together.

The *New York Times*'s Hundred Neediest Cases fund was still needy; almost nobody was sending in checks. It was going to be a sad Christmas for a lot of poor and invalid people.

The skaters in Rockefeller Center were few and far between, and those who were there skated grimly around and around the rink, instead of cutting figure eights or trying out fancy new turns and jumps. They were hardly worth the bother of looking at. A block away, at Radio City, there was almost no line at all for the great Nativity Christmas show live on stage. Unheard of! One of the joys of Christmas is standing on line at Radio City in the cold, knowing what's awaiting you inside.

And, of course, not one snowflake fell.

Cindy Mills was about to lose her marbles. She had a deadline for some heartwarming story to go on the air Christmas Eve, and so far she couldn't find a single person whose heart was warm. She had tried everybody. A sweet-faced little kid in a woolen cap with a bobble on top had told her mournfully that he wasn't getting any toys this Christmas, because his father was out of work. A street vendor in a sharp leather jacket said he was hardly doing business at all, even though his prices were lower than any store. Nobody seemed to want anything. A lady collecting for charity had snapped into the camera that she was sick and tired of standing on a street corner ringing her bell and nobody putting in a dime. Not to mention that her bunions hurt.

What had happened to love and joy and giving and sharing and family and friends? What had happened to the Christmas spirit? Was Cindy going to have to face the camera and tell New York that in a city of more than eight million people, Channel Three News couldn't find a single person whose story was worth telling at Yuletide? It was unthinkable, but it seemed to be exactly what was in the cards.

* * *

MEANWHILE, POPPA AND ROBBIE WERE WORKING THEIR way downtown in a bumpy old cab, fighting traffic. They had looked Renta Santa up in the phone book, and its address was somewhere in the West Twenties, on the ragged fringe of the garment district. Strictly low-rent. Poppa was not being his usual exuberant self; he stared out the window, his face troubled. He'd thought that this case would be a snap—over to Bellevue, spring the angel, and *poof*! Christmas spirit by the sleigh-load. But he'd underestimated the problem, seriously underestimated it.

The city was worse than he could have possibly imagined, and the angel had skipped to even Heaven didn't know where. And time was running out, for Christmas, and for Mike Halligan. There was so much at stake here, not the least of which was that he didn't want to check out with an unsolved case, leaving Robbie disappointed in the old man. Robbie's belief in Poppa was maybe the most important thing in Poppa's life. How could he leave his grandson with the memory of his grandfather's failure? How could he leave his city in this condition? What kind of detective was it who failed when he was needed most?

Robbie saw his grandfather's sad face and respected his silence. But he put another interpretation on it, a natural one. He knew that Poppa had only a couple of days left, and then he'd be . . . gone. And Heaven was very far away, and when Poppa went there, it would be for keeps this time. He moved across the seat and slipped his small hand into his grandfather's.

"Are you scared, Poppa?"

The man turned and smiled gently at the boy. "A little." Then he put his arm around Robbie's shoulder and pulled him close in a long, silent hug. Yes, he was scared. Apart from everything else, he didn't want to go. He wanted to stay and watch Robbie grow up, help him with his problems, teach him from his own experience how to get on in the world.

"Isn't there any way you can get out of going back?" asked Robbie hopefully. "I mean, I've seen you do some pretty fast talking."

Poppa chuckled, shaking his head. "I don't think there's any way this time."

"What if we hid?" asked Robbie with the logic of a nine-year-old.

Poppa gave the boy's shoulder an affectionate squeeze.

"Hey, we got these extra days to be together. Most people don't get a chance to come back and be with someone they love. At least I don't think so."

Robbie bit his lip so that he wouldn't cry. This was the hardest thing he'd ever had to face, even harder than Poppa's "death." That, at least, had been a fact when it was presented to him. He hadn't had a chance to say good-bye. There'd been no hope at all. This time, he would have to make his mind up to it *before* it happened, and how could he do that? How could he of his own free will say good-bye to Poppa?

"It won't be the same without you," he said miserably. "I remember how I felt when I thought you were dead."

The old man nodded thoughtfully. "I was angry, too, but they know what they're doing up There. I've had time to think about it. I'm one of the lucky ones. I lived a full life, and I wasn't a burden on anyone."

Now Robbie couldn't control the tears anymore, and he hid his face in his grandfather's shoulder and wept.

The cab was bumping down Seventh Avenue, through the racks of garments being pushed through the streets by sullen workers. The racks were filled with colorful summer dresses, incongruous in December, but that's the rag business. Trucks were double-parked in no-parking zones, unloading new merchandise that nobody wanted to buy and that would bring the retailers a loss. Drivers were banging on their horns, and the air was filled with the curses of angry cabbies and jeering truck drivers.

They drove past 34th Street, and Robbie leaned out to see if he could catch a glimpse of the Empire State Building, but it was two long blocks east, on Fifth Avenue, and traffic was bumper-to-bumper, so no luck.

As you probably have guessed, things were pretty quiet down at the Renta Santa office. Any other year at this time, the phones would be jumping off their hooks, and Murray, the owner, would be hiring Santas by the dozens. But just look at today. Two days before Christmas, two of the Santas were still sitting around the office, playing cards in their shirt sleeves, and the phone hadn't rung but once, and that was a wrong number, a Puerto Rican lady wanting Maria Concepción.

But now the phone was ringing again, and Murray was on it like a mutt on a Milkbone, snatching it up before it got to the second ring.

"Renta Santa," he said through the chewed wet end of his cigar. "Fifteen bucks an hour, minimum three hours, flat hundred you get Santa for the whole day." He listened a minute. "Uh-uh. You either pick him up or pay the cab fare, both ways. When d'ya need him? In an hour? You plan everything this far ahead? Yeah, yeah . . . gimme the address." He scribbled on a pad that sat balanced on a Styrofoam cup of stale coffee. "He'll be there. Listen for the sleigh bells."

Murray swiveled in his chair to look his stock over. He had one fat Santa, one thin one. The fat one, Calvin, was a jolly-looking black man whose belly filled out his Santa costume naturally. The skinny one, Ed, was a white man with a sour face, who had to use a pillow stuffed down the front of his red trousers. His sour expression wouldn't show much once he got the beard on.

"Hey, Calvin!" yelled Murray.

"Yeah?" The black man smiled, showing a gold front tooth.

"What gives?" complained Ed in a thin, querulous voice. "I was up next."

"You want the job?" Murray asked Ed. "It's yours." Now it was Ed's turn to smile.

"It's up at the Mystic Knights Lodge Hall, 126th Street and Lex." Murray finished with an evil smirk.

The light dawned. "That's *Harlem*!" squeaked Ed.

Calvin gave a booming laugh from the bottom of his mighty belly. "Yeah, sounds like I better handle this one." He stood up and pulled on his Santa jacket, grabbed up his wig, beard, and hat, and went ho-hoing out the door just as Robbie and Poppa walked in.

Murray yelled after Calvin, "Try and not spill anything on the suit this time!" Then he turned to the newcomers. "What can I do for you? Need a suit for Christmas Eve, huh?"

Shaking his head no, Poppa pulled out the mug shot. "You know this guy? His name's Wiley Boggs."

The photograph provoked an immediate and excited reaction. Murray jumped up out of his chair and even took the cigar out of his mouth, a first.

"Yeah! Yeah! I know him, the bum! I sent him out to Zeilbach's Toy Store two days ago! He never showed up there, and he never came back! He's still got my suit! You know where he is?"

"No," answered Robbie innocently, "but your suit's in the police ward at Bellevue."

"You got anything on him?" persisted Poppa. "A phone number, address?"

A disgruntled Murray jammed the stub of the ancient cigar back into his mouth. "Nah... he walked in off the street like the rest of them." Gesturing toward Ed, he lowered his voice to a whisper. "These guys don't have phones or addresses."

Now Poppa employed a time-honored, never-fail police method. He opened his wallet and took out a ten. Money talks; everybody walks. "My name's Halligan," he told Murray. "I'm staying at the Mayflower, on Sixty-fifth. If, by chance, he shows up here, give me a call. I'll make it worth your while."

Nodding, Murray pocketed the sawbuck and scribbled down Mike's name and address.

It was a very disappointed pair that left the grungy old five-story building that housed Renta Santa. Their only lead, and it had evaporated into thin air! No address, no phone number for Boggs; where, in one of the biggest cities in the world, were they going to find an escaped angel, especially one with powers, who didn't want to be found?

They were stumped, and they knew it.

Poppa made a fast phone call to an old informant of his, to get the word out on the street that Halligan was looking for a guy named Wiley Boggs, who was possibly claiming to be an angel. Fifty bucks and no questions asked. It might bring them some information, but more than likely they'd come up empty. Angels didn't hang around the underworld, waiting to be spotted by the cops. At least no angels that Poppa had ever heard about.

It was time to check in with Los Angeles again, to tell the Westins that all was still well (a fib) and that they were having a wonderful time (another fib) and not to worry.

But there wasn't any answer. The phone rang and rang, and Poppa hung up and called the number again, just in case he'd misdialed, and he let it ring about fourteen times, but there really *wasn't* any answer. Reluctantly, they hung up.

"I wonder where they could be," said Robbie. He was a little homesick, and disappointed, because he needed to hear his mother's voice. Or his father's. Even Missy's voice would be acceptable at this moment.

Poppa looked at his watch. "Well, it's only four-thirty in L.A. We'll call them later from the hotel."

Harry, Mike's street squealer, was waiting for them in the lobby of the Mayflower. He was a small man, unshaven and disheveled, but with an astonishingly lovable face, one of nature's permanent innocents.

"Sorry, Mike." He shrugged after the two men had exchanged affectionate greetings. "No one on the street knows nothin' 'bout this Boggs. What's his scam?"

Poppa thought a moment. "That's the problem. I don't think he has one." He reached into his wallet and slipped the other man a five. "Thanks, Harry."

But Harry held up his hand and pushed the money away. "For nothin'. It was good seein' you again, Mike. I really mean it. It was just like old times."

Robbie waved and Mike smiled as Harry went out the revolving door.

"What now?" asked the boy.

"Now chow. Let's go get us some dinner."

CINDY MILLS HAD BEEN HAVING THE SAME KIND OF frustrating day that Robbie and Poppa had been going through, and for much the same reasons, although she didn't know Wiley Boggs. She and Jim had driven the Channel Three van all over Manhattan, out to Queens (which was usually good for a heartwarming story), over to Staten Island (which until today hadn't failed her), and all to no avail. They hadn't shot a frame of usable footage. There was no little old lady without a home, taken in by a loving family out of Christmas kindness; no down-and-out bum who picked up a winning lottery ticket; not even a mongrel with a red ribbon around his neck adopted from a shelter for some poor kid's Christmas present. Even in the Italian neighborhoods, which start getting ready for Christmas shortly after Easter, the decorations were lifeless and slipshod. Nobody seemed to have anything to tell the camera except complaints and grumbling. They hadn't seen one smiling face, or heard one happy voice.

Although she had a keen nose for news and her analyses were usually right on target, Cindy couldn't put her finger on what was wrong. Blame the City Council, blame the weather, blame the economy, blame the Grinch, and you still didn't really have the reason that Christmas was going to be a dud. If she didn't know better, she'd say that there was some kind of higher reason behind all of this . . . as though somebody up there didn't like us. *I must be getting punchy*, she thought. *Too many tight deadlines. Next, I'll be hearing voices telling me to save France.*

It was getting late, and she was very tired and low in spirits. Better get the van back to the station and try again tomorrow. After all, tomorrow was Christmas Eve, and things had to get better. If there was any Christmas spirit left in the world, it was bound to come out on Christmas Eve. Right? An early start; they'd get an early start. There had to be a Christmas story out there somewhere, and if there was, Cindy would find it.

Cindy stopped to pick up some groceries, intending to eat an early dinner alone and get to bed by ten. But when she let herself into her warm, bright apartment, with its tree decorated lovingly from top to bottom, and put a cassette of Christmas carols on the stereo, she felt ashamed of herself. Here she was, looking for Christmas spirit all around town, when she didn't have any in her own heart! Dining alone, when downstairs Mrs. Honeywell sat all by herself, an old woman with no family at this time of the year, nothing to do but stare at the TV? Instantly, she ran lightly down one flight and knocked on the old woman's door. When she mentioned dinner and saw Mrs. Honeywell's face light up, Cindy's own spirits lifted. *This,* she thought, *is what Christmas should be all about. This is the story I ought to be looking for. People with people. People feeling for others, instead of only for themselves. I hope it's out there.*

POPPA HAD BEEN PRETTY SILENT ALL THROUGH DINNER. He'd taken Robbie to a favorite old restaurant of his, with sawdust on the floor and brass lighting fixtures, green glass windows, and good hamburgers. But when the burgers and thick steakhouse fries arrived, Poppa only nibbled. He was turning the case over and over in his mind, looking for a lead, for some opening that could bring him to a resolution of this case. After all, he'd been a detective for many years, and a damn good one. Was he so rusty now that he should give up? No, something was eluding him, something important. If he could only pin down what that something was . . . that all-important tiny clue . . . he could show Robbie and the Arch

Angel and everybody else that Mike Halligan still had what it takes.

Robbie watched Poppa and kept quiet. He was pretty smart for his age, and he had a fair idea of what must be going on in his grandfather's head. He only wished he was older, could be more helpful. He chewed his burger, hoping for inspiration, but nothing occurred to him.

Mike paid the check, took a toothpick out of the little china holder by the register, and gave it to Robbie. Then he tucked one in his own mouth, and they went out through heavy polished revolving doors.

They were in midtown, on Fifth Avenue. It might as well have been the Mall back in the Valley, only colder. No, thought Poppa, even the Mall had some life to it. Not like this.

"I'm having a great time," Robbie said, putting his hand on his grandfather's arm. "Really."

Poppa wanted to cry at the kid's loyalty. He was such a fine little boy.

"But you're not seeing what I wanted you to see. And it's all that damn angel's fault! Oh, you've got to be here when it's all decorated and lit up! The streets should be filled with shoppers! People ought to be singing carols on the street corners!" Poppa shook his head, distressed.

But something had been on Robbie's mind for a couple of hours, and now he asked the question that had been bothering him.

"Poppa, what did you mean when you told Harry that Wiley 'doesn't have a scam'?"

Poppa's mind was still on the problem, but he gave Robbie an automatic answer. "Huh? Oh, all criminals have a scam. They—" He broke off as the significance of what he was saying sank in. This was it! This was that tiny something that had been eluding him, the little clue that might unlock the case. His face lit up with excitement, and his eyes danced.

"Wiley Boggs isn't a criminal; he's not even a *person*. He's an *angel*!"

Robbie didn't understand. Why was his grandfather suddenly so excited? "What's the matter, Poppa?"

But Poppa was on a roll. Nothing could stop him now. He'd been on the right track after all, just on the wrong train. All this time he'd been trying to put himself in Wiley Boggs's place, just as when he was on the force he'd always been able to put himself in the place of whoever he was after. That was his great talent. But Wiley wasn't mortal and that's where Poppa had made his mistake. Immortals and mortals don't think alike.

Grabbing Robbie by the hand, he broke into a trot. "To catch an angel, you have to think like an angel," he told the boy.

Robbie felt a glow as he ran by his grandfather's side. He wasn't sure how, but something he said had given the old man an idea. He wasn't so little and useless after all.

"Where are we goin', Poppa?" he asked, but Poppa was saving his breath.

It was only three blocks to St. Patrick's Cathedral, but Poppa was wheezing a little by the time they got there. He had pointed out the church to Robbie on their way to dinner, telling him what a fine cathedral it was, how sometimes he'd taken his Mary and Robbie's mother, Kate, there to Mass on Sunday, and how wonderful midnight Mass at Christmas was, with the choir singing carols and the church lit up by a million candles. Because Poppa's beat was the midtown area, St. Patrick's had been like his parish church, and he loved it, not only as a great New York City landmark but as the place of his personal worship.

Robbie was surprised to see that they were going inside. Wow! He'd never been inside a church as big as this one. The church they attended in the Valley was made of redwood, and it was ranch-style, like their own house. This was something very different, walls of stone supporting graceful pillars and arches that soared toward Heaven and probably got there. It was the most beautiful, most peaceful, and most fragrant place that Robbie had ever seen, and he tiptoed after Poppa, unwilling to break the silence.

At the holy water font, Poppa dipped his fingers in and made the sign of the cross over himself, and Robbie followed suit. He crossed himself again at the head of the aisle, and the boy genuflected beside him. Then Poppa walked toward the high altar, a look of exaltation on his face. Toward the sides of the richly draped altar were tall candle stands bearing many candles, lit and unlit, and collection boxes for the poor. Poppa lit two candles; the first was for his dead wife, Mary, and he spoke a silent prayer for the repose of her soul. The second was a candle for his intention, and he asked God to let him find the angel and bring joy back to the city. Then he put a ten-dollar bill in the collection box and took Robbie by the hand.

"If anyone on earth knows about angels, it's Monsignor Donoghue," he whispered to Robbie, and the boy felt suddenly reassured by his grandfather's confident tone.

"How do you know him?" whispered Robbie back.

"Monsignor Donoghue was my parish priest. I was about your age when he came to St. Barbara's. He was fresh out of the seminary. He straightened a lot of us kids out; our part of Brooklyn was tough." He stopped and smiled, remembering. "I met your grandma at one of his church dances. And he married us five years later."

"Does Mom know him?" Robbie wanted to know.

"Who do you think baptized her?"

"Well, I hope he can help us," whispered Robbie.

"He will, Robbie, he will."

Only a handful of worshipers were praying in the pews

as the two left the church, and their footsteps sounded very loud in the boy's ears. He hated to disturb their prayers, but the worshipers didn't even look up, as they were lost in their own thoughts.

The parish house for St. Patrick's is around the corner from the cathedral, an oasis of peace in bustling midtown. The rectory is built of stone, and inside all is polished wood paneling and soft lighting glowing from antique glass-globed lamps. Robbie had never seen so many oil paintings before, or such beautiful ones. Cherubs, saints, the Mother and Her Child; he didn't know the names of the artists or have any idea of how very precious—near-priceless—were these paintings in their heavy gilt frames, but he was awed nevertheless.

It smelled different in here—he could make out the smell of furniture polish and wood smoke, but the boy didn't recognize the characteristic scent of beeswax from the heavy candles that stood in silver candelabra on the long marble tops of the carved credenzas. In one paneled room, Robbie caught a glimpse of tall library shelves filled with leather-bound books, their tops gilt. It was to this book-lined room that they were ushered. A fire crackled cheerfully in the fireplace, and leather chairs, dark and deep, stood around as if waiting for visitors.

But Poppa didn't sit, and neither did Robbie. The old man stared expectantly at the door, and in a few minutes it opened and two men came in. Poppa uttered a soft exclamation and took a single step forward.

The man who opened the door and escorted the other through it was tall and young. He wore a black suit and a white priest's collar, and in the firelight his cheeks seemed very red and healthy. But it was the other man, the old man who walked so slowly, leaning so heavily on a cane, who caught Poppa's and Robbie's attention. His body was very lean and bent and, in the long black silk cassock he was wearing, appeared so delicate as to be almost evanescent. His face was lined with many wrinkles, the skin almost paper-white, but the eyes were still young and bright, snapping with intelligence and curiosity.

When the old priest stopped and smiled at Poppa, the smaller man darted forward and kissed the thin gnarled hand with its heavy veins. But, as Poppa straightened up, the Monsignor caught him around the shoulders, and the two men embraced silently, tears in their eyes.

"Well, and what kind of trouble are you in now, Michael?" asked Monsignor Donoghue playfully, with just the hint of an Irish brogue. "It must be important to rouse an old priest out of bed."

But Poppa said not a word; he simply stared at the Monsignor.

"Aren't you going to say anything?" snapped the old man. He was at least eighty years old, and very frail. Poppa was remembering his vigor, so many years ago, when a young Father Patrick Donoghue would tuck his cassock up, belt it, and kick a football across a vacant lot with the swiftest and strongest of the kids. So many memories, so very long ago.

"Are you just going to stare at me?" The Monsignor was torn between annoyance and amusement, but he could understand Poppa's silence. "Yes, I know I've aged." He turned to throw a pointed look at the young Father Karl, who was hovering protectively in the background.

"It's because they treat me like an old man. Never let me do anything for myself."

And, in fact, Father Karl came forward now to lead the old priest to his favorite leather wing chair and settle him comfortably in it. The old man peered into the room, his eyes shadowed in the firelight.

"Who's that hiding back there?"

Now Poppa found his tongue. "It's my grandson, Robbie." He gestured for the boy to come nearer. "Kate's boy."

Father Karl was handing Monsignor Donoghue his bifocals, and the old priest slowly tucked the earpieces around his ears and adjusted the glasses on his bony nose.

"Come closer, lad. Let me get a look at you."

Robbie approached with tentative steps, completely awed by the ancient majesty of this man. He couldn't possibly imagine him as a parish priest taking care of mundane duties. He pictured him doing only heavenly tasks.

The priest stared a long time at the boy; he was moved almost to tears. He saw standing before him the image of the child Michael Halligan, that feisty little street hoodlum he'd had to take in hand so often so long ago. The same clear eyes, the same snub nose, the same red hair.

"Doesn't look anything like you, Michael," he said at last. "A lot handsomer than you were at that age." Both men smiled, knowing the truth of it.

"Father Karl . . ." The old man turned in his chair. "Fetch the boy some milk and cookies."

The young priest left, closing the door softly behind him. Father Karl understood that the Monsignor wanted to be left alone with Halligan so that they could talk.

"Now," said the Monsignor, settling back in his chair, "how about a little refreshment for us?" He gave Michael a wink. "Remember where it is?"

Only a split second, then Poppa remembered. "St. Thomas Aquinas's *Summa Theologica*?" he asked.

The old priest nodded, and Poppa walked quickly over to one of the bookshelves and ran his hand along the spines of the books. When he came to the fat, well-read copy of St. Thomas, he pulled it gently off the shelf, careful of its precious venerability. There, behind it, sat an almost full bottle of Irish whiskey.

Robbie gave a small shout of delighted excitement.

"Just like Poppa! Except at home he hides his behind the—"

"Robbie!" cried Poppa warningly, but it was a beat too late. The kid had spilled the beans.

Robbie's face turned brick red, and he shut his mouth tightly. But the Monsignor just laughed. Where in the New Testament did it ever say that a man who'd worked long and well for most of his days was not entitled to a wee drop of the water of life? He watched Michael take two glasses of finest crystal from the silver tray that stood on the marble top of the credenza, and he called out a gentle warning.

"Don't be stingy."

Michael added an ounce more John Jameson to each glass and handed one to the Monsignor, who took an appreciative sip and leaned back in his chair.

"Now, tell me. What brings you here?"

Poppa took a gulp of the whiskey and waited until he could feel its fire warming his veins. Then, with a deep breath, he said, "What would you say if I told you I died, went to Heaven, and was sent back to find a missing angel?"

There was a long minute of silence, almost unbearable to Robbie, in which the two men looked deeply into each other's eyes.

The Monsignor saw in Michael's face the little boy

he'd known first and the man he'd later become. A man who never told a lie, whose life was dedicated to eradicating as much that was evil and wrong as he could, a good husband, a good father, a good Catholic. Michael's eyes met his clearly, with no hesitation, no evasion, no embarrassment.

In the old priest's eyes, Poppa saw no mockery, no laughter, not even any amazement, just calm assessment and a peace of soul that betokened utter trust.

"I'd say," said Monsignor Donoghue, "that I'd like to hear the whole story."

So Mike told him everything. The trip they'd planned, he and Robbie; how he'd gone up the ladder with the lights; the awful knifelike pain in his chest; the ascending ray of light and the unearthly music; the people on the line ahead of him (the old priest made a sympathetic sound when Poppa talked of the 35-year-old jogger); the angel with the computer printout (the Monsignor chuckled out loud); how the Arch Angel had made a deal with Poppa to find Wiley Boggs; how he'd come down to earth and had been, of course, disbelieved by everybody except Robbie (the Monsignor threw the boy an approving glance that made Robbie wriggle with pleasure); how they'd come to New York on the trail of the missing angel; how Wiley Boggs had given them the slip at Bellevue; how the trail was cold; how Poppa had come to the rectory for the Monsignor's help because of his realization that he wasn't equipped to think like an angel. Then he fell silent, waiting for the priest to speak.

By now, the Monsignor was shaking his head in total amazement. Never had he heard a story like this one, so filled with wonders, yet so convincingly told. And if ever there was a mortal who would argue with angels, if there was ever a mortal who would turn his back on Heaven to keep a promise to a little boy, that mortal was Michael Dennis Halligan. But Michael was eyeing him expectantly, waiting for him to speak, so the Monsignor cleared his throat and leaned forward in his chair.

"I've always believed in the concept of Heaven," he began slowly, "but I must confess, I thought the order of angels was only theological myth." Lowering his voice, he looked at Michael eagerly. "Was there really a gate?"

Poppa nodded. "Yes, and it was just about my turn to pass through, but I remembered my promise to Robbie, and . . ." He turned in his chair to look at the boy he loved so much. ". . . I'm really gonna miss that kid." Then he turned back to Monsignor Donoghue and forced a grin.

"Yeah, all that stuff you preached about Heaven wasn't crap—" He caught himself and stopped short, but the old priest hadn't seemed to notice the slang. He was still musing over Mike's extraordinary story.

"It's comforting to know," Monsignor Donoghue replied, "because I shall be seeing it myself soon enough."

Then he sighed, wondering what advice he could give this man who had come seeking it so hopefully.

"As for finding that angel...It sounds like an almost impossible task." The two men nodded at each other somberly.

Then the old priest's wrinkled face brightened and his eyes took on a mischievous twinkle.

"I wouldn't be surprised if they had another reason for sending you down," he remarked.

Poppa leaned forward in his chair, all ears.

"What do you mean?"

But the old priest shook his head, and the light in his wise old face dimmed a little. "I don't know for sure," he told Michael. "But you'll know when the time is right. I wish I could help you, but..." He shook his head hopelessly.

"You can, Father," said Poppa in a low voice. "Will you hear an old friend's last confession?"

The Monsignor looked fondly at Michael. How many men, already guaranteed Heaven, he wondered, would think of a last confession now? *Not many, I'll wager. Not many.*

"It would be an honor, Michael," said the priest quietly and with love.

Poppa slipped to his knees and bowed his head for the priest's benediction.

"Bless me, Father, for I have sinned. . . ."

SIX

CINDY MILLS SAT IN THE NEWS EDITING STU-
dio, running videotape. Her fingers were poised
over the control board, and occasionally she'd press
a key to freeze-frame, holding an image on the
large color monitor so that she could study it more
carefully. At other times, she'd fast-forward, scru-
tinizing the action that moved rapidly across the
screen like a silent movie run at the wrong speed.
When she got to the part of the film she wanted,
she'd rewind a few frames and watch it at normal
speed. She'd been doing this for three hours now
and was getting pretty tired, also discouraged.

The footage itself was beautiful and even inspiring, the very essence of the holiday spirit. A sequence of joyous images, a montage of happiness. Children's faces illuminated by laughter as they gather around Santa Claus; an old people's home visited by carolers; skaters in long mufflers whirling around the Central Park rink; the giant Christmas tree at Rockefeller Center, all lit up; a pile of toys being delivered to an orphanage; a kitten in a Christmas stocking; a family sitting down to a holiday turkey dinner, with all the fixin's; an airport crowded with weary but cheerful travelers arriving home loaded down with presents; The Salvation Army serving Christmas dinner to the needy; a church choir sending a beautiful *"Ave"* up to Heaven.

"That the stuff you got today?"

Cindy turned to see her boss, Mel, looking over her shoulder at the monitor.

"Hah! Don't I wish!" said Cindy in a tone bitterly sad. "No, this is *last* Christmas's tape. I pulled it from the file." She shook her pretty head mournfully. "It's like a different city this year."

Mel glanced over at the studio clock. It was after eight in the evening.

"Hey, what are you still doing here?" he asked her. "I thought you went home."

Cindy reached over to the console and pressed the POWER OFF button. Then she switched off the monitor and gathered up her purse and gloves.

"I *did* go home!" she exploded in exasperation. "But I couldn't get this damn assignment off my mind! I've spent two days looking for a usable story, and I haven't found it yet. I want to know why! I want to know why New York City isn't New York City anymore! So I came back here to check and see whether I remembered it right. And I did! New York is always *wonderful* at this time of the year. I wasn't imagining it; it's exactly as I recalled it. Something is very different and something is very wrong here. It's as though the spirit has gone out of this town, leaving nothing but an emptiness and a kind of wordless anger. I hate it!"

Mel's eyebrows shot up; he was startled by this outburst from a person as steady and as usually unemotional as Cindy.

"Well, hate it or love it, tomorrow night is Christmas Eve, and I have to put something on the air for the human-interest spot. I gotta have a story."

"Don't worry. You'll get it," said Cindy a little grimly. Striding quickly over to the coat rack, she took down her sheepskin coat and long muffler. She gritted her teeth as she struggled into her coat. "You'll get it if I have to go out there and wrestle one to the ground with my bare hands!" Then, with a dramatic toss of her muffler, she was out the door and gone.

ROBBIE HAD FALLEN ASLEEP IN THE CAB GOING HOME from the Monsignor's, and Poppa tried not to wake him as he lifted him gently from the taxi's seat and carried him in through the hotel door. In the elevator, the boy opened his large blue eyes, but the light was too much for them, and they closed again, his long, silky lashes casting shadows on his freckled cheek.

But Poppa had to put Robbie down to get the key out and open their room door, and the boy, half-awake, asked drowsily, "What time is it?"

"Past your bedtime. And you've had a long day."

"But we've got to find Wiley," protested Robbie groggily.

"First, we got to get some sleep," Poppa told him tenderly. He fumbled in his jacket pocket for the bulky hotel key.

"We going to call home again?" asked Robbie in the middle of a yawn.

Poppa turned the key in the lock and opened the room door.

"Yeah, we should. And I hope your father's calmed down by now."

"He hasn't!" said a grim voice inside the room.

And the light was snapped on, revealing a very angry Rick Westin, an anxious Kate Westin, and Missy Westin, trying to keep her teenage cool.

Uh-oh, said Poppa's glance at Robbie.

Uh-oh, said Robbie's glance at Poppa.

The jig appeared to be, as they say, up.

* * *

AFTER THE "DISCUSSION," WHICH WAS MUCH MORE OF an angry lecture on the part of Rick and an uncharacteristic silence on the part of Poppa, with occasional little clucks of conciliation at both of them from Kate, everybody went to bed.

Robbie was carried off to the "safety" of his parents' room, where Rick could keep an eye on him; he didn't trust Poppa as far as he could throw a baby grand piano. The Westins had taken a two-room suite with a rollaway bed. Missy slept on the living room couch, and Robbie on the rollaway next to his father's side of the bed.

Alone in his room, Poppa stared into the darkness and tried to think like an angel until sleep overcame him.

Breakfast the following morning was something of a tense and uncomfortable meal. They met in the Mayflower coffee shop, and all of them crowded into a large corner booth for six near the window. Rick made certain that he sat down between Robbie and Poppa so that there could be no collusion between the guilty pair.

Kate ordered coffee and black toast; Missy, who was perpetually on a diet to go from skinny to skinnier, wanted only black coffee but, after a few sharp words from Kate, grudgingly accepted half a grapefruit and a whole-wheat English muffin without butter. Rick had his usual high-protein, low-fat, high-fiber perfect breakfast of bran cereal, banana, skim milk. Poppa ordered breakfast ham and two fried eggs, over easy, and Robbie, who always wanted whatever Poppa had, did the same.

When the eggs arrived, swimming in grease, Poppa smacked his lips and reached for the salt shaker.

"No!" Kate scolded, taking it out of his hand before he had a chance to use it. "You shouldn't even be having the eggs."

Poppa shrugged mildly and picked up the ketchup bottle instead, dousing the gooey yolks with liberal gobs of the red stuff, then mashing the yolks into the sauce and swirling them around.

Missy, grossed out, turned her face away, but Rick exclaimed with disgust, "How can you eat that?"

"Hey, Poppa! Finished with the ketchup?" Robbie reached a freckled hand across the table for the bottle, but Rick grabbed it out of Poppa's hand before the Heinz reached Robbie.

"Just eat your eggs," he ordered tersely. Robbie, in enough trouble already, meekly fell to.

Poppa, also on his best behavior, put down the thickly buttered white toast he was mopping his eggs with and picked up his fork.

Rick took a mouthful of his All-Bran and munched it carefully before he spoke. "I'm going to check with the airlines and see if any of them can get us out of here today." He put his spoon down neatly and started to leave the booth.

"Rick!" Kate cried, stopping her husband. "Maybe Dad's right," she said persuasively. "We're here, and tonight's Christmas Eve. Why don't we stay and try to salvage something out of all this nonsense?"

Rick looked across at his wife, and it was apparent that he was hesitating.

"Yeah," breathed Missy, coming to life. "Then I could do some shopping."

"Please, Dad," added Robbie, his little face full of hope.

Rick looked around the table at every eager face, his eyes coming to rest at last on Poppa.

"Rick, I've apologized," said Poppa in a soft voice. "I'm sorry I caused you all this trouble. I'm sorry you had to come in from California." He cast down his eyes and said with finality, "But it's over." And only Robbie knew what he meant.

Now Poppa looked up, his eyes meeting Rick's, and they reminded Rick of Robbie's eyes, so round and blue and trusting. Now the eyes were pleading.

"All I wanted was to show Robbie Christmas in New York. And we're all here now, so let's enjoy ourselves."

The old man turned toward his daughter, and his face was alight with excitement. "Have you ever told him about our family tradition? The carriage ride up Fifth Avenue and through the park?"

Kate returned her father's smile, and her lovely face

softened with the nostalgic memories of happy past Christmases.

"I'm sure I have," she told her father softly, touching his hand. "Rick, please, come on... please?"

Every eye was turned on Rick, and it would have taken a stronger man than he to stand up under the barrage of pleadings. At last he let his breath out in a long and exasperated sigh, and looked sternly at Poppa.

"No more tricks?"

Poppa shook his head meekly.

"You don't leave our sight?"

Poppa shook his head again: total surrender.

"And not another word about angels?" Rick knew he had the old man over a barrel, and Poppa knew it too.

Mike raised his hand to swear on his life, not another word about angels, but before the words passed his lips, the coffee shop hostess, carrying menus, came up to their table.

"Excuse me, Mr. Halligan?"

Poppa looked up. "Yeah, that's me."

"There's a phone call for you."

A quick look passed between Robbie and Poppa, a tiny flicker of hope flaring up in both glances.

"Wonder who it could be," said Robbie softly, half to himself.

Robbie and Rick stood up to let Poppa squeeze out of the booth, and they watched him follow the hostess to a phone in the hotel lobby. From where they were sitting, they couldn't see him once he'd left the coffee shop.

"He's up to something," grumbled Rick suspiciously.

"No, no, don't worry, darling," said Kate.

Rick lowered his voice so Robbie wouldn't overhear him.

"Okay, we'll stay a couple of days. But remember what we agreed upon. As soon as we get back, we find a rest home for him."

But Robbie *did* overhear the words, and his eyes filled up with tears.

As soon as Poppa heard Murray's gritty voice on the phone, a bit muffled by the soggy end of the cigar, his heart gave a great leap upward.

"He's here, now," whispered Murray hoarsely. "The guy in the picture, Wiley Boggs. He's puttin' on his Santa suit this very minute. I'm tellin' ya, he's nutty as ever. He came in mumblin' somethin' about giving New York one more chance."

Poppa's face broke into a wide Irish grin.

"Stall him. I'll be right there."

As he went to hang up the receiver, Murray's voice came out of it, so loud and so clear that he must have removed the stogy from between his teeth.

"Don't forget the money!"

This is it, the break we thought we weren't gonna get! thought Poppa jubilantly. *Gosh, I hate to run out on them, especially now, when we were all gonna spend the*

*day together, and after I promised to be good. But I can't
help it; Rick and Kate will just have to understand. This
is what I was sent here to do, and I've just gotta do it.
But I better let Robbie know.*

Back in the coffee shop, the Westins were planning
the day, while Robbie kept his eyes glued to the lobby,
trying to catch a glimpse of Poppa.

"Mom, we *have* to go to Saks," Missy was insisting.
"And I *can't* be in New York and not see *Bloomingdale's!*" The thought was beyond endurance; she might
as well die right here, face-down in her uneaten grapefruit.

"You know what this trip has cost me already?!" demanded Rick heatedly. "Kate, you can forget Hawaii this
summer. We've blown our vacation fund."

Poppa appeared in the lobby doorway, and Robbie
caught sight of him. He sneaked a glance at the others;
the three of them were arguing too enjoyably to look up.

Poppa put one finger to his lips, signaling silence.
Robbie nodded imperceptibly. Then Poppa drew a circle
around his head with one finger. A halo. The angel!
Then, a triumphant "thumbs up!" with both hands.

Robbie broke into a grin and jerked a thumb at his
chest, meaning, "Me, too? Can I go, please?"

But Poppa was shaking his head, and holding out both
hands, palms up. He pantomimed, "Sorry, Robbie." And
he was gone in the next instant.

"Missy, your father's right," Kate was saying. "We

can't be spending money like this. There are a lot of other things to do."

"Yes," agreed Rick. "New York's full of museums, and they don't cost anything."

The look on Missy's face was that of total and complete suffering such as no mortal had ever known. Museums were being offered up in place of Bloomingdale's! In the long course of history, had any other human being been put to such torture?

The coffee shop window at which the Westins were sitting looked out onto Central Park West. Only Robbie saw Poppa dart wildly into traffic, yelling for a cab. But because of the holiday, many drivers had stayed home, and all the cabs were taken. Robbie could see Poppa dodging in and out of the lanes of moving traffic, calling and waving his arms, but it was only when he was nearly knocked down by an empty cab, and that cab had stopped with a loud screech of its brakes and a furious blast of its horn, that the rest of the Westins broke off their discussion and looked out of the window to learn what all the noise was about.

And there was Poppa, jumping nimbly into the back seat of the taxi and driving off!

Kate gasped and Rick turned to Robbie with an accusatory glare.

The boy smiled weakly. "He raised his hand," he explained. "But he never *swore....*"

* * *

THE STORY HAD COME TO CINDY IN THE MIDDLE OF THE night. Going home from the studio yesterday evening, she'd stopped for some Chinese takeout food and had eaten alone with the television set off. Not even the eleven o'clock news. She wanted to be by herself, with only her own thoughts, to piece together something that could be put on the air Christmas Eve. She was a young woman who took her work very seriously, and this elusive story was preying on her mind. How could she be this close to deadline in a city the size of New York and not be able to pull it off? The writer O. Henry had found a short story filled with warmth everywhere he'd looked, and Cindy could find nothing. Was it her fault? Were her perceptions off?

She washed up the single plate and her pair of bamboo chopsticks, put the empty container into the garbage and the garbage into the steel can outside her kitchen door, and went to brush her teeth and wash and cream her face.

But once in bed, she couldn't sleep. The story—or, rather, the lack of the story—kept pounding at her, giving her no peace. Finally, she decided to take a warm bath to relax her and allow her to sleep. As she drowsed in the steamy little bathroom, almost sleeping, the idea came out of nowhere and hit her. At once, she was wide awake!

In ancient times, the mathematician Archimedes once had a very complicated problem set to him by the king of Persia, and he discovered the solution while taking his bath. He ran out into the streets, wrapped in the ancient Greek equivalent of a towel, shouting "Eureka!"—which in ancient Greek means . . . eureka. Cindy did none of those things. She dried herself off, sat down at her dressing table to scribble some notes on her idea, brushed her hair a hundred strokes, and went to bed, where she curled up with a smile and slept like an infant for eight and a half hours.

The following morning she arrived at the studio fresh as a rose, a spring in her step and a sprig of holly in the buttonhole of her fur-collared coat. Jim Johnston, her usual minicam operator–van driver, was off for the morning, being a family man and today being Christmas Eve, but she managed to round up Perry Perez and gave him driving instructions for the Riverside Rest Home in the upper Bronx. It was a home for the aged.

All the way there, she burbled her enthusiasm to an apathetic Perry.

"It hit me in the middle of the night. I remembered reading about this guy Pringle a couple of years ago. He was a hundred and three years old then, and the point of the story is that he was born on Christmas Day!"

"Hey, you don't have to sell *me*," retorted a bored Perry. "I'm just filling in for Jim. I'll shoot anything you want."

But Cindy was excited enough for both of them.

"So I called the nursing home first thing this morning, and they told me that Mr. Pringle is still alive and still there with them. Mel is gonna love this! I mean, Pringle is older than the Brooklyn Bridge, if you can believe it. He's going to be celebrating his hundred and fifth Christmas tomorrow!"

The girl's eyes were shining at the thought, the wonder of a life that held so many memories, that spanned a time in which there were no electric lamps up to a time when television was broadcast from satellites in space. It was a miracle in itself, and a wonderful story.

But when they reached the Riverside Rest Home, a very different story awaited them.

Mrs. Bush, the home administrator, met them at the front office, blushing with the embarrassment that ordinary people feel when faced with a media star. It was obvious to Cindy that she'd had her hair and nails tinted for the occasion, just in case the camera would be on her for a split second. But her face held only distress.

"You look just like you do on television, Cindy," she gushed. "I'm Mrs. Bush, the administrator. I tried to reach you at the station, but they said you were already on your way."

Cindy's heart sank. The words and the look on Mrs. Bush's troubled face were an obvious signal. Mr. Pringle, poor man, had died, the day before his birthday! That must be it!

"Is there a problem?" asked Cindy anxiously.

"Yes, I'm afraid so." The woman's mouth twitched nervously, and she glanced over her shoulder.

Cindy bit her lip. "But when we spoke this morning, you said everything was set!" She could feel her story melting away beneath her outstretched fingers.

"It *was* set." Mrs. Bush spoke sympathetically. "As a matter of fact, Mr. Pringle was looking forward to this interview. But then his granddaughter called. They're not going to pick him up tomorrow." She shook her head unhappily. "You see, his family has a reunion every year, to celebrate his birthday and Christmas. He *so* looks forward to it. It's the only time he ever gets to go out."

Cindy was getting the picture, but she could hardly believe her ears.

"Don't tell me they're not having it this year!" she gasped.

Mrs. Bush nodded her carefully coiffed head sadly.

"It seems that not enough of the family members were interested," she replied in a low, embarrassed tone. Then, with another glance over her shoulder to make certain that nobody was overhearing them, she whispered confidentially, "Mr. Pringle's absolutely devastated. He refuses to talk to anyone."

Stunned, Cindy could only stare at the administrator. Here's a man 105 years old, and his family can't even take the trouble to celebrate his longevity once a year!

She was right! Something was terribly, terribly off about this Christmas! People weren't behaving normally! It was as though an *anti*-Christmas spirit was abroad, infecting everybody and everything it touched. A spirit of mean-hearted malice, making people act differently from how they did on other Christmases. It was as though something were... missing! Yes, that was it! Something was *missing* this year, absent, gone away! Was this the story she'd have to put on the air tonight? Please, Lord, no!

She turned away from the nursing home, and Perry shouldered his equipment with a shrug and followed her. Cindy didn't speak a single word on the whole long drive back into Manhattan. Her spirits were lower than they'd ever been. Now she was back to square one, no story. Wrong—she was way *below* square one, because not only didn't she have a story, but she had no time left. Deadline was only a few hours away, if film were to go on the air tonight. Her morale, already at zero, slipped a couple of notches, to minus three, and was falling fast.

Poppa came rushing through the Renta Santa office door like a miniature twister, and if there had been anything in his path, he would have knocked it down.

"Where is he?" he demanded breathlessly.

Murray put down the black Santa boot he'd been polishing and rose slowly behind his desk. He didn't meet Poppa's eyes as he said, "I... ah... I couldn't keep him here. He left."

"What?!" Poppa's voice rose to a high squeak of disbelief and indignation.

"Don't get excited," Murray said quickly and placatingly. "I know where he went. I sent him to an office party uptown."

"Why did you let him go?!" demanded Poppa.

The chief executive officer of Renta Santa shook his head, bewildered. "I don't understand it myself," he admitted. "I don't know why I did it. . . . It just seemed right at the time."

Now Poppa recognized that bewildered expression; he'd seen it on Dr. Ullman's face after she'd sprung Wiley Boggs from Bellevue. It's how you look after you collide with an angel.

"He seems to have that effect on people," he conceded. Couldn't blame Murray. "Where's the office party?"

"Where's the money you promised?" Murray countered. Be-angeled or not, he wasn't *that* far gone.

Poppa put one hand into his wallet, which was a lot less fat than when he'd gotten on the plane in L.A., and pulled out a five-dollar bill.

Murray eyeballed it unhappily. "This is what you call making it 'worth my while'?" he asked in a disgruntled voice.

"You'll get more when I find him," promised Poppa. "Where'd you send him?"

Murray debated a minute, then gruntled up, taking

the fin and shoving it into the pocket of his rumpled trousers. With a finger that had seen cleaner days, he riffled through the grimy cards in his Rolodex file.

"Billing, Blankford and White. It's a law firm. Fifth and Fifty-second."

Poppa scribbled the address down and went out the door as quickly as he'd come in. There wasn't a moment to lose. A law firm Christmas party, with booze flowing freely! No telling what Wiley Boggs might get up to!

Back at the Mayflower Hotel, Rick Westin was still seething. If Poppa weren't too old to spank . . . Here he'd given them all his word, and the very next moment he was disappearing into a taxicab. Damn the old man anyway! He'd spoiled everybody's Christmas! He'd dragged Robbie three thousand miles on some cocka-mamie wild-angel chase; he'd upset Kate and Missy; he'd cost everybody hundreds and hundreds of dollars in air fares and hotel bills, not to mention meals—and all for what? For total senility, that's what! Well, by Heaven, here they were in New York, and if they were going to stay for a while, he, Richard Westin, would be in charge of things, not a crazy old loon who hallucinated angels!

He glared at his children as they buttoned and zipped themselves into winter clothing, which, as southern Californians, they did rather clumsily. Then he shepherded them to the elevator and almost shoved them inside.

"Now, we're going to have a good time, understand?!"
He barked at them like a Marine DI, and both recruits
flinched. "I don't want to hear either of you complain
about anything!" Rick glared hard at Missy. "And a good
time does *not* mean shopping, young lady!"

"Maybe I should stay with Mom," said Robbie hes-
itantly. He really didn't want to go out with his father
and sister. How would Poppa ever reach him if he left
the hotel? What if some new development, something
crucial, arose and he wasn't there to help Poppa? After
all, this was *his* case, too. It wasn't fair! But he didn't
dare let his father see what he was thinking, or he'd be
on the next plane back to Los Angeles.

"You're coming with me!" snapped Rick. "I'm not
letting you out of my sight!" The three of them left the
hotel and stood shivering on Central Park West. They
were on their way to Fifth Avenue, to look at the store
windows. From there, Rick had planned museum ex-
cursions, to stuff a little culture into their youthful heads.

"If your mother wants to stick around the hotel waiting
for that crazy old man to come back," he told Robbie
angrily, "that's her business."

"Poppa's not crazy!" declared Robbie, his cheeks
burning. "He—"

"I don't want to hear another word out of you! You're
in enough trouble as it is!" growled his father.

Robbie subsided, defeated. Somewhere in this city,

Poppa was all by himself, trying to track down an elusive angel without Robbie's help. Robbie was a prisoner . . . well, just about a prisoner.

And the funny thing was that Robbie couldn't tell for sure whether he wanted Poppa to succeed, find Wiley Boggs without Robbie, or fall flat on his face, proving that Robbie's detective skills were as good as Poppa's. A little bit of both, probably. Miserably, he followed his father and sister down toward Columbus Circle. Nothing was turning out the way it was supposed to!

SEVEN

WILEY BOGGS STRAIGHTENED HIS FALSE COT-
ton beard and gave a few uncertain pats to his Santa
Claus outfit. It had been made for a man larger
than he was, and the jacket and trousers fell into
ungainly folds around him. He was chubby, was
Boggs, but cherub-chubby, not fat. Portly and
pinchable.

Directly ahead of him as he stepped out of the
elevator on the thirty-seventh floor was a pair of
imposing double doors made of mahogany, topped
by a broken pediment arch with acorn finial. Very
colonial, very impressive. Founding Fathers and
all that. To one side of the doors was a brass plaque,

brilliantly polished, on which was engraved the name of the firm—BILLINGTON, BLANKFORD & WHITE, ATTORNEYS AT LAW.

Wiley knocked on the door. He waited. Nothing. He knocked again, this time a little more forcibly. Waited. More nothing. Now he balled his pudgy hand into a fist and banged as hard as he could.

After a moment, the door opened, and a man in dirty coveralls peered around it. Behind him, Boggs could hear the angry whine of a vacuum cleaner.

"Yeah?!" demanded the janitor in a surly voice.

"I'm here for the office party," said Wiley politely.

"You're too late!" the janitor grumbled. "It broke up about an hour ago." His words were drowned out by the noise of the vacuum, and all Wiley could make out was "late" and "hour."

"What did you say?"

Reluctantly, the janitor kicked the switch on the cleaner, and it whined down into silence.

"I said, they all went home!"

Wiley took a step into the law firm's doorway and looked for himself. His eyes widened in surprise. The office, which must have been both dignified and impressive earlier in the day, was a total shambles. Catastrophe City. The floor was littered with torn crepe paper and broken light bulbs from the decorations that had been ripped down from the walls. Plastic glasses and paper plates were on every surface, even on top of the water cooler and the coffee machine. The chairs, most of them, had been tipped over and resembled victims of a hit-and-run collision. One desk had been pushed as far as the window, and almost through it, as though somebody had been trying to throw it out into the street.

And that was only for starters. There was torn paper everywhere, even stuck to the ceiling, and it resembled (and most certainly was) important legal documents. The handsome desks of heavy walnut were stained and scarred by wine and whiskey spills and overturned ashtrays.

Wiley gave a little whistle of astonishment.

"It looks like it was quite a party! Why did it break up so early?"

"Party?" snorted the janitor. "Maybe that's what it was supposed to be, but no one was in the mood. Ol' man Billington had a little too much to drink and told Blankford what he thought of him." Just remembering it, the cleaning man shook his head, laughing. "Oo-wee! He let go of forty years of hate! Then ol' White stepped in and they both jumped all over him. The whole shebang turned into one big brawl. The employees seemed to be having a wonderful time; at least, nobody stepped in to break it up." He shook his head again, and his grin grew wider. "That's the last Christmas party *this* company will ever see!"

Wiley looked around the room ruefully, feeling very guilty. He recognized in this mess of breakage and litter his own defection. Christmas spirit was what had been missing from this party, and that was all his fault. What could he do about it now, though? Here it was, Christmas Eve already, and this was a city of millions of people. Where could he start to make things right? His angelic heart sank in his cherubic breast.

"Here," said the janitor, bending down into the litter and picking up a half-filled bottle of whiskey. "Merry Christmas."

He held the bottle enticingly out to Wiley.

Wiley Boggs put his hand up to push the bottle away, then he hesitated. Christmas was lost, wasn't it? He was in plenty of trouble Upstairs already, wasn't he? Could he be any worse off than he was? Probably not. If he had a drink or two, would he feel better about things? Almost certainly. So what choice did he have?

So the rejection became an acceptance, and the bottle passed between the two men.

"Merry Christmas," said Wiley, but his guilty heart wasn't in it.

GETTING AROUND THE CITY ON CHRISTMAS EVE WAS A hopeless affair. You could take a train from Penn Station to Philadelphia in less time than it took to get across town. Poppa clenched his fists in frustration as his taxi cab inched and quarter-inched its way toward Fifth Avenue and 52nd Street. If he didn't hurry, the Christmas party might be over and he'd lose Wiley Boggs again. *Although, what if I found him? At the eleventh hour, with less than a day to go, what could anybody do to spread cheer around a city this size? Even an angel?*

Nevertheless, nobody could ever say that Mike Halligan didn't give his all. He'd had tougher cases to solve, and he'd pulled them off, although he was never under the gun like this time.

He had only one day left . . . to live. There! He admitted it. He had only until tomorrow and then back on that golden escalator to admit defeat. What would he have accomplished when that Arch Angel would be looking at him so sternly? He'd taken Robbie with him, to show the boy what Christmas in New York was like. And had he? No, he'd failed. He'd been sent on a mission—find a missing angel and bring back Christmas spirit. And had he? Let's hear it one more time. No, he'd failed.

Well, as long as there was life in his body, Poppa Halligan was not going to admit defeat! He learned forward and tapped the cab driver on the shoulder.

"Faster!" he ordered. "Can't you go any faster?"

The driver didn't even bother to turn around.

"Sure, Mac," he said sarcastically. "I can flap my

wings and fly like a boid, highhhh over all de cars and buses. Will dat suit ya?"

Everybody's a comedian, thought Poppa, and he sank his head into his hands.

RICK HAD SIMMERED DOWN QUITE A BIT AS HE AND HIS children walked down Fifth Avenue from the Plaza Hotel. Missy kept running ahead to look in all the store windows, catching her breath at all the top-label designer merchandise with the fancy price tags. They were heading downtown, in the direction of St. Patrick's and Saks, of Lord and Taylor and Altman's, and it was their plan to stop off at the Empire State Building, on 34th Street, and go up to the Observation Deck, even though the day was so overcast there might be little to see.

Neither Rick nor Robbie had any interest in the windows, but instead were in deep conversation on a most important topic—Poppa.

"I think it's wonderful that you love your grandfather so much," said Rick more gently to his son. "But you have to realize that when people get older, they . . . well . . ." He searched for the most delicate way to put it. ". . . They change."

But Robbie was not fooled by Rick's choice of words.

"Poppa's not crazy!" he maintained stoutly. "I can't explain it to you, 'cause you'll never understand."

This didn't sit too well with his father, but Rick decided to ignore the implicit criticism.

"Your grandfather is living in the past," he told Robbie patiently. "He's in love with a New York and a Christmas that just doesn't exist anymore. He—" Rick broke off as something caught his attention, something that made him scowl in anger.

"Look! Just look at *that*!" he exclaimed angrily, pointing.

Robbie turned to see what his father was pointing at. A man in a Santa Claus suit was coming out of an office building, holding a bottle of whiskey to his lips for a slug. His white beard was pulled to one side, but the bottle obscured his face.

"*That's* Christmas in New York!" said his father scornfully.

They kept walking, past the Cathedral, where Poppa had lit the candles and where Monsignor Donoghue had heard his confession. They were at Saks now, and Missy was as lit up as a firecracker.

"*Please*, Daddy, can we just go in and *look*?" she begged.

Yet Robbie kept staring back over his shoulder at the Santa, something tugging at the back of his mind.

"All right," conceded Rick. "But *just* to look."

As Rick followed his daughter through the revolving door, the Santa finally pulled the nearly empty bottle away from his face.

Robbie gasped, remembering the mug shot. It was Wiley Boggs! It *was*! The angel himself! Oh, where was Poppa?!

"Come *on*, Robbie." Hearing his father's voice, the boy hesitated, not knowing what was the right thing to do. He had promised his father that he'd be good, and he was, after all, only nine. So he followed the Westins into the revolving door.

But as the door turned around, Robbie came right out again. He'd made up his mind. Whatever trouble he'd get into (and he was sure he'd catch Hail Columbia for this) his loyalties were with Poppa and Heaven. As little as a nine-year-old boy might be able to do, that little he would do!

Wiley was still staggering around Fifth Avenue, but he had reversed his direction and was now heading north, uptown.

Now, you have to understand a few things about the way that traffic moves in New York. Almost all the avenues are one-way, and so are just about all the streets. The avenues run north and south; the streets run east and west. The odd-numbered streets go west; the even-numbered go east. Bear in mind that Poppa was coming *uptown* from the West Twenties, where the offices of Renta Santa were. You can't go uptown on Fifth Avenue, because it's one-way downtown. So he was heading up Madison Avenue.

In order for Poppa's cab to get to 52nd and Fifth, where he hoped to find Wiley Boggs at the lawyers' party, the cab would have to head west on 53rd Street, then downtown on Fifth. So keep this picture in your head. Wiley Boggs, emptying the bottle as fast as he could, was reeling uptown on Fifth, followed by Robbie, while one block over on Madison, Poppa was grinding his teeth in a cab and saying, "Only two more blocks!"

We now come to the intersection of Fifth Avenue and 53rd Street. Wiley was headed north just as Poppa's cab passed the same corner, going west to make a turn on Fifth.

But Poppa didn't see Wiley. He was so pressured that he was looking at his watch just as Wiley stumbled past his cab. The cab stopped for the red light, and Wiley, who had the pedestrian green signal, wobbled on by.

When Poppa looked up from his watch, he saw . . . Robbie!

"Robbie!" yelled the old man just as the light turned green and the cab jolted forward.

"Hold it! Lemme out of here!"

The cabbie put his foot on the brake and the taxi jolted forward, almost sending Poppa flying into the front seat. He managed to get the door open, reached into his pocket, and threw some money at the driver without waiting for change. He could see Robbie up ahead, and in order to catch him, he ran against the red light. All around him, brakes screeched and horns honked angrily at the foolish old man who had nearly gotten himself killed.

"Robbie!" he yelled again, almost catching up to the trotting boy.

His grandson turned, and his small face brightened in a big, relieved smile.

"Poppa! Boy, am I glad to see you!"

"What are you doing? Where are you going?"

Robbie pointed proudly to the wobbly figure in the red suit only about five yards ahead of them.

"I'm tailing Wiley Boggs!"

Poppa's eyes bugged out in amazement.

"What?! Where'd you find him?"

"He came out of an office building, drinking. Dad, Missy and I were sightseeing...."

For the first time, Poppa realized that Robbie was all by himself. "Your dad, where is he?"

Robbie swallowed. He wasn't sure whether to be proud or ashamed. A little of each, he guessed.

"I ditched him," he confessed.

Back in Saks, Rick was frantic. People were pushing and shoving in all directions, but no sign of a small redheaded boy. Rick had searched up and down the aisles, out in the street, and back in the store again. He *knew* Robbie must be in the store somewhere; hadn't he seen him coming through the revolving door? He'd been right behind Rick. Where could the boy have gone?

Missy, her shopping interrupted, was nothing but annoyed. How should she know where the little pest was? Imagine coming three thousand miles to shop at Saks and spend the time looking for your little *brother*. . . . It was to slit your wrists!

THERE WAS NO MORE THAN ONE SMALL SWIG LEFT IN the bottle. *One small swig for angel, one big drink for angelkind*, thought Wiley, feeling distinctly silly and a whole lot better. He wobbled a little on the balls of his feet, weaving forward and back like one of those toys you can't knock over. The people around him were giving him the hairy eyeball, outraged at such a public spectacle of drunkenness on the part of St. Nicholas, but Wiley neither noticed them nor cared.

He lifted the bottle to his lips, and it almost got there, when suddenly, he felt himself being grabbed by the shoulder of his Santa suit and spun around.

"I beg your pardon," he said with inebriated indignation.

He was staring into the rather pugnacious and very Irish face of a small man accompanied by a smaller, freckle-faced boy. Both of them were regarding him somewhat grimly.

"Wiley Boggs, right?" demanded Poppa.

Wiley tilted back on his feet (a rash move) and squinted down at Poppa through bloodshot eyes.

"You have the advantage of me, sir. Who are you?"

"He's a detective!" the little boy cried out, excited. "The Arch Angel sent him down . . . to find *you!*"

"I sh—sh—shouldn't be shurprised . . ." hiccuped the angel. His head was beginning to hurt and his tummy was feeling very rocky indeed. Little men in dirty boots were dancing a Virginia reel on his tongue. "So now that you found me . . ." he inquired, one hand to his throbbing head, "what are you shupposed to do?"

Poppa took a quick look around. Halfway up the block, between Fifth and Madison, he could see a coffee shop, the lights on. It was open. "Let's go in there. We better get you some coffee."

Grabbing Wiley firmly by the arm so that the angel couldn't give him the slip, he guided him toward the coffee shop, Robbie bringing up the rear of the guard.

"Two coffees," said Poppa to the counterman, "and . . ." He looked inquiringly at Robbie.

"A hot chocolate," said the boy.

The three of them sat down on stools, Poppa making sure that the angel sat on the stool furthest from the door. It was sober-up time, and Wiley was going to drink black coffee until it came out of his seraphic ears. And if Poppa had to hold him down and ladle it in, well, that's the way it would be.

Only a couple of stools away, Cindy Mills sat, dejectedly making little puddles in her black coffee with the bowl of her spoon. On the stool next to her sat Jim Johnston, her regular minicam operator, who, while sympathetic to the girl's plight, was still philosophical enough to know when he was licked.

"It's no big deal," he was telling her persuasively. "You pick up the phone and say, 'Mel, we ain't got it. There's no human-interest piece for your six o'clock news.' Simple. That's all there is to it. Hey, it's Christmas Eve. I'm goin' home." He picked up his counter check and started to get up from the stool, but Cindy put one pleading hand on his arm.

"Oh, come on, Jim," she begged, looking very pretty, although she was unaware of it. "Don't *you* give up. We'll find a story. I mean, you can't tell me that in all of Manhattan there's not one upbeat item."

Jim shrugged his capitulation. He wasn't hard to persuade, not when Cindy was doing the persuading.

"Okay, you stay here, and I'll load the van. Pick you up in five minutes. But just for that, *you* pay for the coffee." And he threw his check back down on the counter.

Cindy grinned in agreement. Good old Jim! She smiled at the counterman, whom she knew, this coffee shop being one of the regular Channel Three haunts; the studios were right around the corner, on Madison.

This was it, the last ditch. *Once more into the breach, dear friends, once more*, she quoted to herself. If she couldn't get the story on this try, she'd give up and phone Mel.

She glanced idly around the coffee shop. Nothing much going on except an old man and a boy trying to sober up an obviously drunk Santa Claus with black coffee. No story there!

* * *

Kate sat, forlorn and miserable, in the small suite at the hotel. She'd been waiting for hours by the phone, and not once had it rung. Nothing about Dad, and she was more worried than ever. Alone in this city, and maybe even—for the first time she admitted to herself that Rick might be right after all—maybe even a little senile. So many things can happen to dotty old men in a big city like this. He could simply walk in front of a bus! Who knows what?

She had tried to watch television to get her mind off Dad's disappearance, but the images on the screen were just that, flickering images with no meaning, and she didn't even bother to stand up, walk over, and turn the damn set off. It muttered in the background, with nobody to watch it or listen to it.

She picked up a magazine and riffled through the pages, seeing nothing. But every nerve in her body was standing up and screaming, so when she heard Rick's key turning in the lock, she jumped off the sofa and came running toward him.

"Not a word on my father!" cried Kate before Rick could get a syllable out. "I've spoken to Captain Santini twice in the last hour."

When Rick didn't answer her, Kate took a second look at him; his face was anxious and guilty. She turned to look at her daughter; Missy looked terribly nervous. Kate felt a sudden churning in her stomach as she realized that Robbie wasn't with them.

"What's the matter?" she gasped, her cheeks pale.

"Don't get excited," Rick began, realizing that his words were hardly calculated to calm Kate down. "I've already been to the police . . . but Robbie's disappeared."

"Disappeared!" screamed Kate. *"Disappeared?!"*

It took both Rick and Missy to get her to the couch and sit her down. Kate kept trying to reach for her coat so that she could run out into the street and look for them. Her father! Her little son! Both of them! Gone, both of them!

MEANWHILE, THE TWO OBJECTS OF KATE WESTIN'S anxiety were still pouring coffee down Wiley Boggs's gullet. An hour or so had passed—it had grown darker outside—and Wiley was not yet sober; still, he wasn't that far from it anymore. He'd sobered up some and could, with some prodding from Poppa and Robbie, make fairly intelligent conversation.

Wiley was telling them how all of this had come to pass.

"I came down like I always do, to spread the Christmas cheer. I've been doing it for more than a mortal lifetime."

"How do you do it?" Robbie interrupted curiously. "How do you spread the cheer?"

A smile touched the corners of the angel's lips and grew, spreading to cover his entire face. "Oh, it's easy," he told the boy. "A kind word here, some encouragement there. My favorite is to find someone particularly grumpy and turn them around. All it takes is a little smile or maybe a word or two that makes them feel good about themselves." Now the excitement was getting to him, and the angel began to speak more quickly, his words tumbling over each other in their rush to get out.

"It's contagious! It spreads quickly, from person to person, block to block, neighborhood to neighborhood. Then, before you know it, the whole city's got the spirit!"

But the angel's exaltation faltered and faded, leaving only sadness in its place.

"But not this year," he said quietly and sadly. "Nothing seemed to work. . . ." He gave a shrug. "So I gave up!"

"And started drinking," said Poppa with no small sarcasm.

"Hey, I'm not perfect!" Wiley, stung, became defensive. "I *tried*! I was even going to request a *white* Christmas for the city!"

Robbie's little face fell in disappointment, and Poppa took a long, hard look at the delinquent angel. Then he squared his shoulders.

"You've got too important a job to do!" he scolded firmly. "You can't give up! You've got to pull yourself together! There's still time."

But Wiley Boggs was shaking his head slowly from side to side. A seraphic tear as iridescent as a tiny pearl, formed in his right eye and rolled its slow path down the angel's cheek.

"It's impossible," he sighed. "It's too late. It's Christmas Eve . . . and no one cares."

The three of them fell silent, and it became a little later, a little darker outside.

But Mike Halligan wasn't licked yet. He gave the angel an encouraging prod in his heavenly shoulder.

"You *can't* give up!" he shouted. "People are just people, but *you're* an angel! If *you* lose the spirit, what hope is there for anyone or anything else in the world?" He was fighting mad now, Irish through and through.

But the angel still shook his head. "Please leave me alone," he sniffled, brushing the tear away. "You can tell the Arch Angel you did your job. You found me. And you can also tell him that I couldn't do mine."

He got down off the coffee shop stool, a pathetic figure of a broken immortal, and started for the door.

Not knowing what else there was to do, Poppa started

after him, but Robbie caught him by the hand.

"Poppa..."

The man turned. "Huh?"

His little grandson was looking at him earnestly, his brow furrowed in thought.

"It doesn't sound that hard..." Robbie said tentatively.

"What?"

"What he does... making people feel good. It doesn't sound like you need any kind of angel powers. So... if you don't think it's too late... maybe *we* can do it." And he smiled up at his grandfather with all the love in his innocent little heart.

Stunned, Poppa could only stare at his grandson. *Out of the mouths of babes! And a little child shall lead them* were the phrases that came unbidden into his memory. He leaned down and hugged Robbie, really tight, without a word.

"What's the matter?" asked the boy, his voice muffled by the hug.

With mounting excitement, Poppa said, "I've been trying to figure out what Monsignor Donoghue meant. He said that when the time was right, I'd know why I was sent back." He kissed his grandson lovingly on the forehead. "I think you just gave me the answer."

The boy grinned happily up at his grandfather, hugging him back with all his might.

Then Poppa stood up and, taking Robbie by the hand, pulled him off the stool.

"If that misguided angel won't do it, *we* will!"

EIGHT

THE CHANNEL THREE NEWSROOM WAS BUZZ-
ing like a hive of angry bees, the hum growing
louder every minute. This was a sure sign that the
news would soon be on the air, this last-minute
drone of activity. It was five-forty now; by the time
the studio clock's hand stood perfectly vertical
at six and the Six o'Clock News was broadcast,
the newsroom would be almost silent. Only late-
breaking bulletins of monumental importance
could interrupt the format of the program.

Like the captain of a battleship under fire, Mel
was here, there, every-which-where, now on the
bridge, now checking for damage below decks. He

173

went from department to department, making last-minute inquiries to see that everything was ready. So far today, he hadn't seen or heard from Cindy, nor had he looked at a frame of her footage. Where was Cindy, and where was the film she was supposed to have shot?

Mel sent an all-points-bulletin throughout the studio, and an assistant soon brought him breathless news.

"Cindy just called in," said the assistant, a small young man with a weak chin and a clipboard filled with papers. "She hasn't got any tape, but she wants to go on live."

Mel scowled. "With what?"

The young man just shrugged. She hadn't said.

Mel thought fast. This was unprecedented and could result in a horrible few minutes of dead air. "We got anything else for her spot?"

"Um, maybe we could extend sports...."

On the other hand, "dead air" might be pretty lively, and Mel did have faith in Cindy's intelligence and judgment. Besides, who wanted to watch a long sports segment on Christmas Eve? The captain drew a deep breath and issued orders from the bridge.

"Put her on."

SUPPOSE IT WAS YOU WHO HAD TO SPREAD THE SPIRIT on Christmas Eve. Where would *you* begin? I thought so. And that's exactly what Poppa and Robbie did. They picked a corner where pedestrian traffic seemed particularly heavy—Fifth Avenue at 49th Street—and began to sing a Christmas carol. They raised their voices in song, beginning with "It Came Upon the Midnight Clear" and continuing with "O Come, All Ye Faithful."

You probably remember that, back in fourth grade, Robbie wasn't allowed to sing. He was what was called "a listener," because his croaky little voice wandered so far away from the tune that it needed a map and compass to find it again. What you didn't know is that Robbie came by his off-key voice honestly; he inherited it from his grandfather. So the two of them stood there, mouths open, happily murdering Christmas. It was enough to make a cat laugh. Unfortunately for the pair, no cats were passing Fifth Avenue and 49th Street just then, only a lot of people who either ignored them or glared at them for polluting the air with those awful voices.

Only ten minutes of "singing" convinced them that whatever they were spreading, it wasn't the Christmas spirit. They wandered off in search of something else.

"So the singing didn't work," said Poppa, trying to cheer Robbie up. "Let's find someone really grumpy and try to 'turn them around,' as Wiley said."

Well, given the situation, finding somebody really grumpy shouldn't have been too difficult. Almost everybody on the street was wearing a sour expression. But it had to be the right person.

Suddenly, Robbie pointed. "How about her?"

Poppa took a look. "Her" was a bag lady, one of those homeless women who carry around all their meager possessions, usually no more than a few castoff rags, in either a shopping cart with broken wheels or a couple of paper bags. The deposit law, which says you have to pay a nickel deposit on every can or bottle of soda or beer, has been a boon to these derelicts. Lots of people don't bother to bring back the empties but chuck them in the trash. But twenty of those empties times a nickel apiece makes a whole dollar, enough for a cup of coffee and a couple of sinkers, if you don't leave a tip.

This bag lady was picking through the trash in the litter baskets, every now and then coming up with an empty bottle or can, tucking it away in the rubbish she was toting around, her precious possessions.

And boy, was she ever grumpy! Muttering under her breath into her chin whiskers, shaking her fists at imaginary enemies, mumbling curses at the passersby, she was grump on wheels. Turn *her* around and you would be accomplishing a Christmas miracle.

Poppa accepted the challenge. "Perfect," he said to Robbie.

Walking right up to her, Poppa turned on the old Irish charm and flashed her the old Irish grin.

"Hi, there! I just wanted to wish you a merry Christmas!"

The old lady looked up from her trash picking and saw Poppa. What the hell? Didn't he know that this was *her* territory and *her* litter basket? Who did he think he was, trying to muscle in on her turf?

"Buzz off!" she snarled.

Strike two.

CINDY FELT FLIP-FLOPS IN THE PIT OF HER STOMACH that she hadn't felt since her early days in front of the camera. She was having all kinds of second thoughts. Why on earth had she told Mel she wanted to go on *live*? Why on earth had he let her? She had a fair idea of what she wanted to say, but she wasn't sure anybody would want to listen to her downbeat message.

"Ten seconds, Cindy," called Jim.

Cindy nodded. She had selected Rockefeller Center with its backdrop of skaters, the Prometheus statue, and the huge Christmas tree to broadcast live from. She knew it would *look* good on the air, but how her segment would *sound* was a different matter.

Jim held up five fingers, then four, then three . . . He was counting down the seconds before she went on the air live. Two. Cindy took a deep, deep breath. . . .

POPPA AND ROBBIE WANDERED DISCONSOLATELY WEST, heading in the direction of Rockefeller Plaza, where the Christmas tree and the skaters were. Maybe they'd have better luck there. Fifth Avenue didn't appear to be conducive to spreading Christmas cheer. Besides, they'd be killing two birds with one stone, because hadn't Poppa promised Robbie back in L.A. that they'd be making this very trek? Only then, it had seemed like so much fun. Now they were getting discouraged, and Time seemed to be ticking off the seconds for them. Five, four, three, two . . .

In the control booth back at the studio, Mel sat glued to the monitor. Cindy looked good but nervous with the camera on her. Only two seconds before she went on live. One, and *now*!

"Good evening," said Cindy Mills, live from Rockefeller Center. "I'd like to say, 'Merry Christmas,' as it *is* Christmas Eve, but somehow it doesn't seem appropriate, and I'll try to tell you why.

"Yesterday morning, Channel Three's news producer sent me out to find an upbeat story for this segment. Well, it sounded like fun, and not very difficult. This reporter had the same assignment last year and brought back hours of tape filled with happy New Yorkers, sharing joy and good will. It was heartwarming and reaffirming. It made one eagerly await the next holiday season."

Mel frowned at the monitor. "Where's she going with this?" he wondered out loud. So far, the so-called "story" wasn't taking any definite direction.

As they reached Rockefeller Center, Poppa and Robbie saw a very pretty girl bundled into a sheepskin coat, looking directly into a television camera and speaking into a microphone. Intrigued, they drew closer, joining the crowd that had formed around her, and listened to what she was saying.

"Well, it's here . . . but the spirit is missing," continued Cindy. "I've been all over New York, looking for those same wonderful moments of people sharing . . . smiling faces . . . laughing children . . . all those things that symbolize Christmas. But I couldn't find them anywhere. Instead, I saw mean, inconsiderate, downhearted people who didn't seem to care that Christmas had arrived."

She paused to draw breath, but before she could begin again, a voice from the crowd around her yelled, "*I'll* tell you what's wrong!"

Thrown off by the interruption, Cindy fumbled to regain her train of thought. "Ah . . . maybe . . . the problem's . . ." She looked startled as she saw a smallish man, holding the hand of a little red-haired boy, detach them both from the crowd and head purposefully toward the camera.

When you're live on camera, the bane of your life is the people who want to "get on TV," who wave into the camera and make obscene faces and say hello to their families, all the time you're trying to report some tragedy like a fire or a murder. And here were two more of the same, heading right for her. Cindy's heart sank. This was all she needed.

In the control room, Mel's face was etched into a

permanent scowl as he watched this segment on the monitor. Cindy's stock, which a minute before was high, was plummeting fast.

"What-the-hell-is-this?" he growled, all in one word, as he saw an old man and a boy coming into camera range. "Who are they?!"

His assistant shrugged. "I don't know. Maybe she planted them?"

Cindy regarded the intruders nervously. "Excuse me, sir," she said to Poppa. "But this is the Channel Three News, and we're on *live.* . . ."

Poppa nodded vigorously and leaned forward to the microphone in Cindy's hand. "Good!" he said briskly. "'Cause I want to answer your question. I *know* what's wrong!"

Mel rolled his eyes up to Heaven. "Quick! Go to Weather!" he ordered.

The studio camera zoomed in on Weather, and the monitor showed the meteorologist not ready for the first time in his career. The maps were hanging sideways, and his sound assistant was still trying to mike him, although something appeared to be wrong with the mike. A little Heavenly intervention perhaps?

Anyway, "Can't go to weather!" said the assistant, and Mel groaned and put his head into his hands. The Six o'Clock News seemed to be sinking, and the captain was going down with his ship.

But Poppa was looking directly at the camera now and speaking strongly into the microphone, and Cindy, overcome by the oddest feeling, stood by and let him. It was almost as though this little man had . . . powers . . . and she thought she heard music . . . no, impossible!

"You all just expect it to happen!" Poppa was saying. "You take Christmas for granted! You think you don't have to do anything! Well, you're wrong!"

His Irish was up now, and Poppa was really cooking. "Christmas is what *you* make it!" he told the world. "Not the other guy, but *you*! I was a cop in this city for forty-five years, and I saw people at their worst. But for some reason, at Christmas they would change. Like magic. Something seemed to pull everyone together."

"Weather's ready," said Mel's assistant.

But Mel waved a dismissing hand at him. His eyes were fixed to the monitor, which showed a small man, his face alight with conviction, pouring his heart out, talking about Christmas. Every now and again the camera would cut to the little boy, whose eyes looked up at the old man as though he were the biggest hero on earth. The camera would also cut to Cindy's reaction, which was one of silent awe. Now the camera was panning through the crowd around Cindy. They were listening, no doubt about it, caught up in what the old man was saying.

"Hold on," said Mel. She had something here, that

Cindy. Why the hell hadn't she told him in advance? It was an irresistible combo—old man, Irish by the look of his mug, former cop, little boy—a Christmas natural.

BACK IN THE HOTEL ROOM, KATE WAS ALMOST IN A panic. They'd been gone for hours, and who knew whether they were even together? It was dark out now, and Kate was certain that Robbie didn't know either the name or the location of their hotel and was completely lost. Only the presence of Captain Santini was keeping her from hysterics. He had men out looking for both Poppa and Robbie, together and separately, and Kate had his assurance that the two of them would be found before too long.

The captain was with the Westins in their hotel suite, Rick and Kate drinking coffee to give them some energy, and the captain smoking one cigaret after another. In the corner, the television set was still playing, and a nervous Missy was half-watching it.

The girl reached out with an apathetic hand and turned the knob to Channel Three, looking for a *Happy Days* rerun. And she gasped! There was Poppa, big as life, and he was looking into the camera and saying, "Sure, some years were better than others. We all have favorites . . . but none were bad. . . ."

And the camera cut away from Poppa, and there was Robbie!

"Mom! Dad!" gasped Missy.

"Not now, Missy," snapped Kate, her nerves as tight as stretched-out rubber bands.

"But I know where Robbie and Poppa are!"

The three adults turned, mystified. Missy was pointing to the television set. Astonished, they drew closer. Poppa was still talking.

"Gosh, I remember coming home from the Pacific, that first Christmas after the war. That was special. It was the first time I saw my baby daughter. . . ."

Kate gasped and burst into tears. His baby daughter! Oh, Dad! Dad! In all this confusion, in all this anger, they had lost sight of the one thing that was most important. How much they all loved and needed one another. At Christmas time and every other time.

Murray and Ed were sitting in the Renta Santa office, depressed. Murray was mad because he couldn't go home, thanks to that Wiley Boggs, who was still out there somewhere with Murray's Santa suit. Ed was depressed because he didn't have any home to go to on Christmas Eve or any other eve.

The small-screen black and white set that Murray kept for idle hours was on, and the two of them were watching it halfheartedly, not paying a lot of attention to the news. But suddenly, their attention was captured and held, by a little man talking about Christmas and what it should mean to everybody. A little man with a familiar face.

"But the holiday season is always special," Poppa was saying. "It's a time to get together and celebrate life! To exchange not just gifts but love and friendship!" He reached down and threw an arm around Robbie, hugging the boy tightly to his side. "That's why I brought my grandson from California. . . ."

The sight of the boy brought Murray's memory into focus.

"Hey, I know that guy!" he told Ed with a nudge. "He gave me a couple of fives. . . ."

Poppa was really into it now, and rolling. He grabbed the microphone out of Cindy's hand. Jim, the camera man, took a step forward to stop him, but Cindy flashed him a signal that said, "Leave this guy alone." This was good television, this was what television should be all about, the genuine excitement of real people, people talking to people, reaching out to people. This was the very meaning of the word "communication."

"But you all let me down!" yelled Poppa at everybody turned into the sound of his voice. "Sure, things have been tough this year! But they've been tough before! . . ."

Cindy stepped out of camera range and joined Jim.

"Stay with him," she told her minicam operator. "I think we got our story."

Jim nodded and zoomed in on the little man's face, which was lit from inside by a mesmerizing glow.

"Hey, I know I sound like some old fool, but just

listen to me!" pleaded Poppa. "I said I know what's wrong, and I do. You all gave up. But it's not too late. There's still time." Excitement was speeding up his words, making his eyes shine. Poppa, recalling Wiley Boggs's words, smiled to himself. "*Smile!*" pleaded Poppa, and smiled at his audience. "*Just smile!*"

Wiley Boggs stepped into a Sixth Avenue bar looking about as far from Heaven as it was possible to get. His Santa suit was stained and rumpled; his beard was on backwards and hung down his back, and somewhere he had lost the red stocking cap with the fluffy white tassel. His shoulders slumped, the corners of his mouth drooped unhappily, and altogether he looked like a most unhappy cherub badly in need of a drink.

"I'll have a martini," he told the bartender. "Make it a double. Not too dry, and . . ."

"Shhhhh!" said three little green elves on the next three stools.

Oh, I gotta give up olives in my martini, thought Wiley. *Now I'm seeing elves.* He took a second look, but very carefully.

He *was* seeing elves. Three little men dressed in green elf suits were nursing three beers at the bar. The suits were spotted here and there with what seemed to be chocolate and raspberry jam, as if they'd been caught up in a food fight in Rumpelmayer's window. What's more, the elves, who had shushed him, had their eyes glued to the color television set above the bar, which was tuned to the Channel Three news. Wiley looked around. *All* the bar patrons were watching TV intently, and so was the bartender, who made no move to mix Wiley the necessary martini.

What the angel was going on here? Wiley squinted uncertainly at the set, trying to bring it into focus. He thought he heard a familiar voice. "Bartender—"

"Quiet! We want to hear this guy!" snapped the elves in unison.

"It's easy," Poppa was confiding to his audience. "Say a kind word here; give some encouragement there. . . ."

Now not only was the voice familiar to Wiley, but the words as well. And the face, too. Wiley recognized the man on camera as Mike Halligan, who'd been sent down by the Arch Angel to find him, Wiley Boggs.

Poppa was getting really excited now, grinning with optimism and the joy of the holiday. "It's contagious!" he was saying. "It spreads quickly, from person to person, block to block, neighborhood to neighborhood. And before you know it, the whole city will have the spirit!" Shouting now, Poppa told everybody, "So we can do it! We can still do it! Do you hear me out there? We can do it!"

Wiley nudged the nearest elf. "That's what *I* told him!"

"Sshhhhhh!"

* * *

THE METEOROLOGIST WAS GETTING IMPATIENT. HIS charts were all in order, his wire was live and working, there was weather outside to be talked about, even if it wasn't going to be a white Christmas, and still he hadn't received the "get-ready" signal from the control booth.

"We're not going to have time for the weather," Mel's assistant warned him, but Mel waved him off. "Just hold tight," he said. This was television in the making, and he wasn't going to lose it now. Tomorrow, this is what people were going to be talking about, the little guy they'd seen last night on Channel Three.

"Now, get up!" exhorted Poppa, his eyes dancing. "Christmas is here! Enjoy it! Hug your parents and children! Go next door and wish your neighbor a merry Christmas! Go outside! Sing! Sing your favorite carol!"

"I love it!" yelled Mel. Good old Cindy! There would be a big raise for her when her contract was up for renewal; he'd guarantee it personally.

Now Poppa turned his attention from the camera to the crowd of onlookers that had gathered about him, drawn by his words and by the sight of the TV camera and crew.

"Come on!" he yelled to the crowd. "All of you! Sing!"

Raising his hand like a baton, he brought it down and began to belt out the first lines of "Joy to the World."

It was predictably awful, but unpredictably effective. Robbie joined right in, the second part of the cat's chorus. Then Cindy came up to stand beside the two and raised her voice in the beloved carol. Hers was a true, clear alto voice as lovely as her speaking voice, and it carried the melody with a purity that was infectious. One by one, then two by two, then more and more, the people standing around joined in the carol. As they did, the TV camera panned over their faces. They appeared to be lit from within, the lines of worry and anger smoothed out by the exaltation of the holy song. Like Wiley and Poppa had said, it *was* contagious! They were getting the spirit, the Christmas spirit.

Wiley Boggs climbed down from his barstool and walked out into the chilly evening. Somehow he didn't seem to want that drink anymore. Besides, the bartender was too busy singing harmony on "Joy to the World" to make it anyway. The three elves had their heads together, belting out the carol, and all the bar patrons were singing with all their lusty might. Christmas had come to Sixth Avenue.

With the microphone back in her hand, Cindy Mills stepped back in front of the camera. Her face was glowing with happiness, and she looked not merely pretty but absolutely beautiful, as though touched by the wing of a seraph.

"As you can see, something wonderful is happening

here, and now I can wish you that merry Christmas. This is Cindy Mills, reporting live from Rockefeller Center. Merry Christmas!"

In the studio control room, everybody was laughing, slapping everybody else on the back, wishing one another a merry Christmas. Joy was everywhere (except in the weather corner).

In the rectory of St. Patrick's Cathedral, Monsignor Donoghue fairly leaped out of his chair with joy. He hadn't been this spry in more than a decade.

"Michael," he laughed at the television set, "you found what it was you were to do!"

Young Father Karl rushed to the old priest's side, concern for the old man's health written all over his face.

"Monsignor, please!"

But Father Donoghue was feeling marvelous, strengthened by this confirmation of his faith in God and man.

"This calls for a celebration!" he laughed to the younger man. "I'm going to teach you the real meaning *behind* St. Thomas Aquinas!" He pointed to the tall bookcase.

"I don't understand," answered Father Karl, perplexed.

"You shall," said the Monsignor with a twinkle in his eye. "Now, just go over to the bookcase. That's right. Find the *Summa Theologica*. That's right. Now, just pull the book out. Gently, boy, gently. That's right. . . ."

* * *

Within a few short minutes, New York City had totally changed. People were ringing their neighbors' doorbells to wish them a merry Christmas. Often, neighbors bumped into neighbors in the hallways, because they were on their way to wish each other Merry Christmas. Decorations appeared out of thin air and were nailed to the front doors and lighted up in the windows. The streets were filled with people singing carols and shoving (although politely and rather happily) into the stores to do their last-minute shopping. They wanted to *buy* things, to give things away to others.

In the Riverside Rest Home, Mr. Pringle, wrapped in mufflers and shawls and with a blanket around his legs, was being bundled into his granddaughter's Buick to be taken home for his 105th birthday-plus-Christmas celebration.

On Fifth Avenue, a passerby thrust something into the bag lady's hand. "Merry Christmas."

The grimy hand opened; in it was a five-dollar bill. The old lady's eyes lit up, and then her toothless face.

"Merry Christmas to you, too, mister!" she called after him. "God bless you!"

And for the rest of the evening, she called out Merry Christmas to everybody who passed by, whether they gave her money or not. Just because it felt so good to say it. And a lot of them did give her money, coins and even bills. She'd have a good hot meal and a warm place to sleep tonight.

Down in the garment district, Murray and Ed had put on the cleanest of the Santa suits and the whitest of the beards and were going through the streets, bellowing Christmas carols. They had picked up quite a contingent of carolers, with more and more coming out of the buildings to join in "Hark, the Herald Angels Sing" and "God Rest Ye Merry, Gentlemen." Seventh Avenue was alive with caroling.

As Wiley left the bar, the elves nudged each other. He looked so forlorn, this would-be Santa. Nobody ought to be alone on Christmas Eve. As one, they hopped down off their barstools and trotted after him, spirits aglow.

The city was magically transformed; joy was everywhere. You could feel it in the air, which, although cold, kissed the cheek rather than nipped it. You could see it in people's faces as they greeted one another, although strangers. The spirit had come back to the city, and not a moment too soon.

Captain Santini had escorted all the Westins into the squad car he'd had standing by at their hotel. With sirens blaring jubilantly, they headed downtown for Rockefeller Center. Robbie and Poppa were bound to be around there somewhere. Not that Kate was worried. It was obvious that the two of them were all right, even better than all right. Poppa had never looked so happy or so healthy, and Robbie, even on the hotel TV set, positively glowed.

Even with the siren, the police car had a tough time getting through. It seemed the entire city was out tonight, bustling happily around, and all of them were heading for the Rockefeller Center area. Why not? There were skaters, and the biggest Christmas tree in the world, all lit up; there were the Fifth Avenue department stores, filled with wonderful things to see and buy. And there was St. Patrick's Cathedral, where the faithful would hear Mass tonight and pray for peace in the world and for the souls of their beloved departed.

Cindy and Jim were wrapping and folding the equipment and loading the van. Cindy knew that television history had been made here tonight, and she was reluctant to leave the scene, reluctant, too, to say good-bye to this wonderful little former cop who had inspired an entire city.

"It's a miracle," she said to Poppa, kissing him on the forehead.

Poppa shook his head. "It's not a miracle," he denied. It's—" He broke off as he spotted Wiley Boggs in the crowd, looking bewildered. Astonishingly, Wiley appeared to be accompanied by the three little green men who'd staged the food fight in Rumpelmayer's window.

"Excuse us for a second, Cindy, but there's someone we have to see." Holding Robbie's hand tightly, he pushed through the happy crowd, accepting pats on the back and rubs on the head, until he reached Wiley's side.

The angel was looking rueful, not a little chagrined, but hardly unhappy to see the pair. "You did it." He shrugged. "I couldn't do it, but *you did*."

"Well." Poppa beamed. "There's still time for you to spread the cheer. Why don't you get going?"

Wiley Boggs looked flustered for a second, but as he searched the faces around him, joyous and loving, he realized that Poppa was telling the truth. There *was* still time. He rushed off. He had a lot of catching-up to do before Christmas morning.

Kate spotted her father and her little boy, surrounded by carolers. Happiness cloaked them; they appeared to be one with the universal spirit. She and Rick pushed their way through the crowd to Poppa, with Missy trailing. And then they were suddenly all together, hugging hard. Robbie and Kate, Robbie and his Dad, even Robbie and Missy, Missy and Poppa, Poppa and Kate.

It was Rick's turn with Poppa, and there was a lot he had to say to the old man, most of it apologetic, all of it affectionate. He'd been wrong, very wrong. There wasn't a senile or crazy bone in Poppa's little body; it was nothing but love and kindness. But before he could open his mouth, one of the elves rushed up to Rick and grabbed him by the pants leg.

"Come on, mister. Sing!"

Rick looked down at the funny little man all dressed

in green. The things you see in New York! He shook his head.

"I've got something more important to do."

"There's nothing more important!" urged the elf. He pointed at Poppa. "Didn't you hear that guy? *Sing!*"

Rick looked at Poppa, who gave him a twinkle that said he understood that words could come later, if they had to. He looked at his wife and his daughter and his little son, all of whom were singing lustily. So what else could he do? Nothing but open his mouth and let his carol join the others'.

"It came upon the midnight clear, that glorious song
of old,
From angels bending near the earth, to touch their
harps of gold.
Peace on the Earth, good will to men..."

And there was good will, to everybody in New York City, thanks to an Irish cop, a little boy, the faith of them both, and an angel who, at the eleventh hour, tried his blessedest and made it happen.

Which, of course, was exactly what Heaven had planned from the beginning, as the Arch Angel found out from Him later, and as Monsignor Donoghue had guessed all along.

* * *

THEY HAD THEIR HOT CHOCOLATE AT RUMPELMAYER'S, with its sweet cap of rich whipped cream, and Poppa drank two. Rick tried to tell him what was in his heart, but the old man took his son-in-law's hand and pressed it, and nothing more had to be said.

There was a line waiting at Grand Army Plaza for the carriage rides down Fifth Avenue, now that the Christmas spirit was upon them again, but the New Yorkers waiting recognized Poppa and Robbie from the Channel Three news, and magically an empty cab was produced for them like Cinderella's coach. It was the best cab, too, with the youngest, proudest horse and the sauciest driver and the sweetest-smelling cushions and blankets.

The Westins and Poppa bundled into it, and down Fifth Avenue they went, clippity-clop. Kate insisted on sitting next to Poppa, just as she had as a little girl so many years ago. The night was beautiful. The gray had disappeared from the sky, leaving it starry and velvety, the kind of sky in which you think you can see Heaven peeping out.

"This is just like I remembered it, Dad," Kate said fondly, hugging her father.

"I'm not too crazy about the way you got us here," said Rick, getting his final licks in, "but I'm glad you did."

Now the ride was over, and they were back again at Grand Army Plaza. They had seen the decorations and the tree all lit up and the skaters crowding the rink, doing all kinds of fancy figures, and people bustling into the stores and coming out with their arms laden with packages tied with bright ribbons. It was Christmas in New York City, and they were seeing it all.

Rick helped Kate and Missy down from the carriage, but Robbie held up his hand.

"Can Poppa and I take a short ride ourselves? Just through the park?"

Rick hesitated, glancing at his watch.

"It's almost midnight, and it's getting cold."

But a look at Robbie's pleading face made his father start to relent, and a quiet nod from Kate clinched it.

"Okay." He smiled. "Just for a few minutes."

"I'll be good," Poppa promised impishly, a boy himself.

Poppa reached up and tapped the driver, and the carriage left the plaza and entered the park.

"Cover up with those blankets!" Kate called after them.

So there they were, only the two of them, just as Poppa had promised back in Los Angeles. A carriage ride in the park for them, and a New York City Christmas. They burrowed down under the blankets. Kate was right; it was getting cold, and the sky was turning darker again, the stars hiding their faces behind gathering gray clouds.

"This has been the greatest Christmas ever!" exclaimed Robbie with a sigh of pure pleasure.

Poppa just nodded; he was very drained and tired, but totally, totally happy and at peace.

"And I learned that Christmas is what *you* make of it," said Robbie with all the wisdom of innocence.

Poppa thought about Robbie's words for a minute, then he turned to his grandson and looked lovingly into his face.

"You know..." he said slowly, as if just coming to the realization himself, "it's not just Christmas. *Life* is what you make of it."

Robbie nodded. Then he flinched slightly as something cold and wet touched him on the cheek. His nose twitched as something cold and wet touched him on the nose. Astonished, he looked up and gasped.

Snowflakes were dancing in the sky, swirling in the light of the street lamps, a white, soft blanket of snow descending. Robbie had never seen anything so beautiful in his life. He reached his hand out to catch a snowflake, but it eluded him. He reached for another and it melted away. But more of them came, and more and more.

"Poppa, it's snowing!" he exclaimed. "It's going to be a white Christmas! Wiley gave us a white Christmas!"

But the old man didn't answer. His head was bent forward as though he were sleeping.

"Poppa?" asked Robbie, his heart in his mouth.

No reply.

And Robbie knew. Poppa had gone back to Heaven. Heaven was a wonderful place, and Poppa would be in eternal bliss, and he'd see Grandma there and everything, but even so, Robbie couldn't stop his tears. The tears mingled with the snow on the boy's face, and Robbie wasn't sure whether it was the weeping or the cold that made him shiver so.

If I'm a good man, I'll see Poppa again someday, Robbie realized. *That's what Heaven is all about. Besides, there'll be plenty of Christmases. We even have them in L.A.! And if I know Poppa, he'll be there, just like Wiley Boggs, to spread joy and show us what the Christmas spirit is all about. Maybe they'll even stop spraying the trees pink.*

At Poppa's funeral, Robbie looked across the sea of mourning faces and saw, without surprise, the cherubic countenance of a completely sober Wiley Boggs. And the angel tipped him the wink.

A deal is a deal.